THE SAFARI KILL

Volume 15: Zen and the Art of Investigation

Anthony Wolff

AuthorHouse™ LLC
1663 Liberty Drive
Bloomington, IN 47403
www.authorhouse.com
Phone: 1-800-839-8640

Published by AuthorHouse 9/22/2014

ISBN: 978-1-4969-3535-9 (sc)
ISBN: 978-1-4969-3534-2 (e)

This book is printed on acid-free paper.

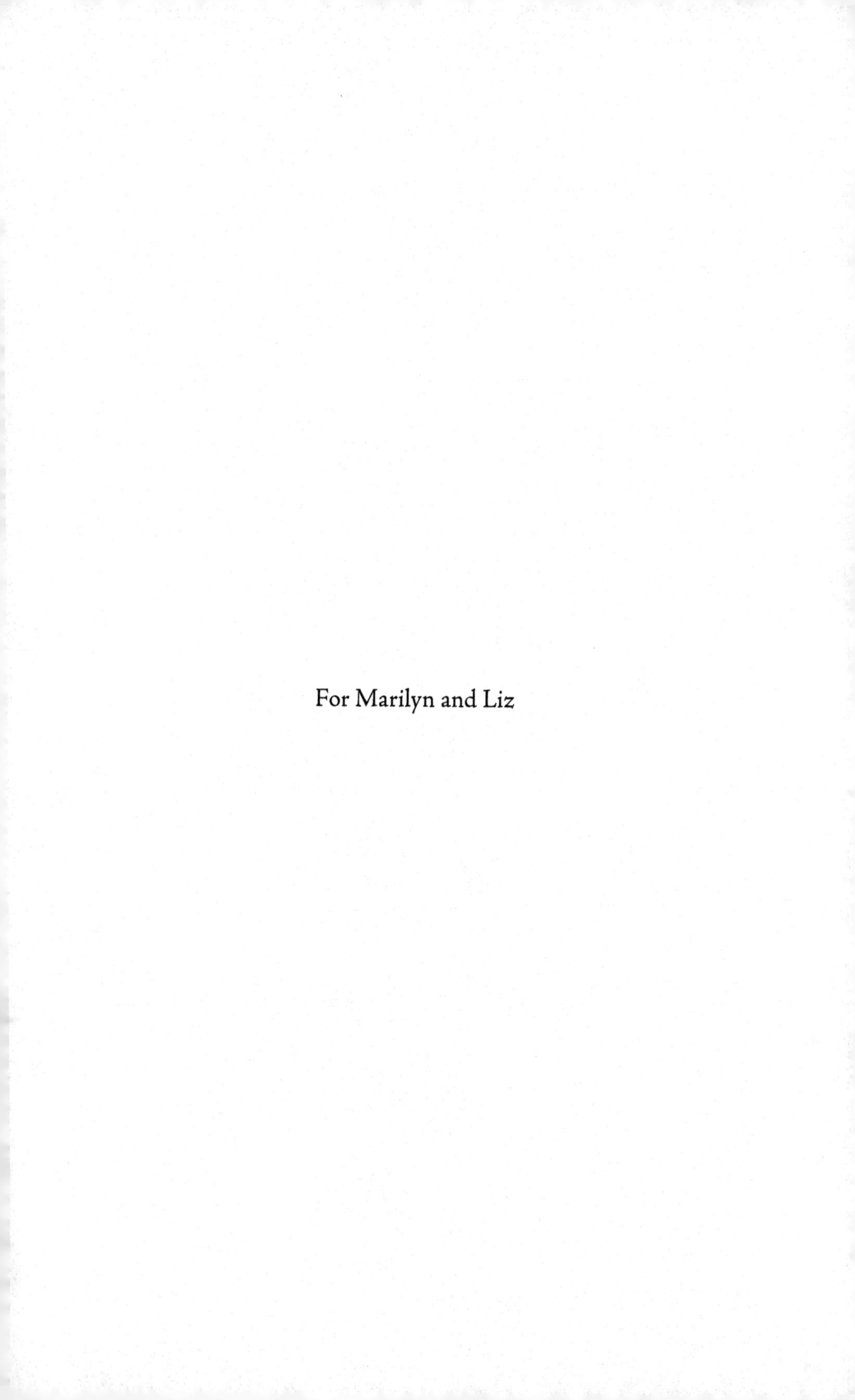

For Marilyn and Liz

PREFACE

WHO ARE THESE DETECTIVES ANYWAY?

"The eye cannot see itself" an old Zen adage informs us. The Private I's in these case files count on the truth of that statement. People may be self-concerned, but they are rarely self-aware.

In courts of law, guilt or innocence often depends upon its presentation. Juries do not - indeed, they may not - investigate any evidence in order to test its veracity. No, they are obliged to evaluate only what they are shown. Private Investigators, on the other hand, are obliged to look beneath surfaces and to prove to their satisfaction - not the court's - whether or not what appears to be true is actually true. The Private I must have a penetrating eye.

Intuition is a spiritual gift and this, no doubt, is why *Wagner & Tilson, Private Investigators* does its work so well.

At first glance the little group of P.I.s who solve these often baffling cases seem different from what we (having become familiar with video Dicks) consider "sleuths." They have no oddball sidekicks. They are not alcoholics. They get along well with cops.

George Wagner is the only one who was trained for the job. He obtained a degree in criminology from Temple University in Philadelphia and did exemplary work as an investigator with the Philadelphia Police. These were his golden years. He skied; he danced; he played tennis; he had a Porsche, a Labrador retriever, and a small sailboat. He got married and had a wife, two toddlers, and a house. He was handsome and well built, and he had great hair.

And then one night, in 1999, he and his partner walked into an ambush. His partner was killed and George was shot in the left knee and in his right shoulder's brachial plexus. The pain resulting from his injuries and the twenty-two surgeries he endured throughout the year that followed, left him addicted to a nearly constant morphine drip. By the time he was admitted to a rehab center in Southern California for treatment of his morphine addiction and for physical therapy, he had lost everything previously mentioned except his house, his handsome face, and his great hair.

His wife, tired of visiting a semi-conscious man, divorced him and married a man who had more than enough money to make child support payments unnecessary and, since he was the jealous type, undesirable. They moved far away, and despite the calls George placed and the money and gifts he sent, they soon tended to regard him as non-existent. His wife did have an orchid collection which she boarded with a plant nursery, paying for the plants' care until he was able to accept them. He gave his brother his car, his tennis racquets, his skis, and his sailboat.

At the age of thirty-four he was officially disabled, his right arm and hand had begun to wither slightly from limited use, a frequent result of a severe injury to that nerve center. His knee, too, was troublesome. He could not hold it in a bent position for an extended period of time; and when the weather was bad or he had been standing for too long, he limped a little.

George gave considerable thought to the "disease" of romantic love and decided that he had acquired an immunity to it. He would never again be vulnerable to its delirium. He did not realize that the gods of love regard such pronouncements as hubris of the worst kind and, as such, never allow it to go unpunished. George learned this lesson while working on the case, *The Monja Blanca.* A sweet girl, half his age and nearly half his weight, would fell him, as he put it, "as young David slew the big dumb Goliath." He understood that while he had no future with her, his future would be filled with her for as long as he had a mind that could think. She had been the victim of the most vicious swindlers he had ever encountered. They had successfully fled the country, but not the range of George's determination to apprehend them. These were master criminals, four of them, and he secretly vowed that he would make them fall, one by one. This was a serious quest. There was nothing quixotic about George Roberts Wagner.

While he was in the hospital receiving treatment for those fateful gunshot wounds, he met Beryl Tilson.

Beryl, a widow whose son Jack was then eleven years old, was working her way through college as a nurse' s aid when she tended George. She had met him previously when he delivered a lecture on the curious differences between aggravated assault and attempted murder, a not uninteresting topic. During the year she tended him, they became friendly enough for him to communicate with her during the year he was in rehab. When he returned to Philadelphia, she picked him up at the airport, drove him home - to a house he had not been inside for two years - and helped him to get settled into a routine with the house and the botanical spoils of his divorce.

After receiving her degree in the Liberal Arts, Beryl tried to find a job with hours that would permit her to be home when her son came home from school each day. Her quest was daunting. Not only was a degree in Liberal Arts regarded as a 'negative' when considering an applicant's qualifications, (the choice of study having demonstrated a lack of foresight for eventual entry into the commercial job market) but by stipulating that she needed to be home no later than 3:30 p.m. each day, she further discouraged personnel managers from putting out their company's welcome mat. The supply of available jobs was somewhat limited.

Beryl, a Zen Buddhist and karate practitioner, was still doing part-time work when George proposed that they open a private investigation agency. Originally he had thought she would function as a "girl Friday" office manager; but when he witnessed her abilities in the martial arts, which, at that time, far exceeded his, he agreed that she should function as a 50-50 partner in the agency, and he helped her through the licensing procedure. She quickly became an excellent marksman on the gun range. As a Christmas gift he gave her a Beretta to use alternately with her Colt semi-automatic.

The Zen temple she attended was located on Germantown Avenue in a two storey, storefront row of small businesses. Wagner & Tilson, Private Investigators needed a home. Beryl noticed that a building in the same row was advertised for sale. She told George who liked it, bought it, and let Beryl and her son move into the second floor as their residence. Problem solved.

While George considered himself a man's man, Beryl did not see herself as a woman's woman. She had no female friends her own age. None. Acquaintances, yes. She enjoyed warm relationships with a few older women. But Beryl, it surprised her to realize, was a man's woman. She liked men, their freedom to move, to create, to discover, and that inexplicable wildness that came with their physical presence and strength. All of her senses found them agreeable; but she had no desire to domesticate one. Going to sleep with one was nice. But waking up with one of them in her bed? No. No. No. Dawn had an alchemical effect on her sensibilities. "Colors seen by candlelight do not look the same by day," said Elizabeth Barrett Browning, to which Beryl replied, "Amen."

She would find no occasion to alter her orisons until, in the course of solving a missing person's case that involved sexual slavery in a South American rainforest, a case called *Skyspirit,* she met the Surinamese Southern District's chief criminal investigator. Dawn became conducive to romance. But, as we all know, the odds are always against the success of long distance love affairs. To be stuck in one continent and love a man who is stuck in another holds as much promise for high romance as falling in love with Dorian Gray. In her professional life, she was tough but fair. In matters of lethality, she preferred *dim mak* points to bullets, the latter being awfully messy.

Perhaps the most unusual of the three detectives is Sensei Percy Wong. The reader may find it useful to know a bit more about his background.

Sensei, Beryl's karate master, left his dojo to go to Taiwan to become a fully ordained Zen Buddhist priest in the Ummon or Yun Men lineage in which he was given the Dharma name Shi Yao Feng. After studying advanced martial arts in both Taiwan and China, he returned to the U.S.

to teach karate again and to open a small Zen Buddhist temple - the temple that was down the street from the office *Wagner & Tilson* would eventually open.

Sensei was quickly considered a great martial arts' master not because, as he explains, "I am good at karate, but because I am better at advertising it." He was of Chinese descent and had been ordained in China, and since China's Chan Buddhism and Gung Fu stand in polite rivalry to Japan's Zen Buddhism and Karate, it was most peculiar to find a priest in China's Yun Men lineage who followed the Japanese Zen liturgy and the martial arts discipline of Karate.

It was only natural that Sensei Percy Wong's Japanese associates proclaimed that his preferences were based on merit, and in fairness to them, he did not care to disabuse them of this notion. In truth, it was Sensei's childhood rebellion against his tyrannical faux-Confucian father that caused him to gravitate to the Japanese forms. Though both of his parents had emigrated from China, his father decried western civilization even as he grew rich exploiting its freedoms and commercial opportunities. With draconian finesse he imposed upon his family the cultural values of the country from which he had fled for his life. He seriously believed that while the rest of the world's population might have come out of Africa, Chinese men came out of heaven. He did not know or care where Chinese women originated so long as they kept their proper place as slaves.

His mother, however, marveled at American diversity and refused to speak Chinese to her children, believing, as she did, in the old fashioned idea that it is wise to speak the language of the country in which one claims citizenship.

At every turn the dear lady outsmarted her obsessively sinophilic husband. Forced to serve rice at every meal along with other mysterious creatures obtained in Cantonese Chinatown, she purchased two Shar Peis that, being from Macau, were given free rein of the dining room. These dogs, despite their pre-Qin dynasty lineage, lacked a discerning palate and proved to be gluttons for bowls of fluffy white stuff. When her husband retreated to his rooms, she served omelettes and Cheerios, milk instead of tea, and at dinner, when he was not there at all, spaghetti instead of chow mein. The family home was crammed with gaudy enameled furniture and torturously carved teak; but on top of the lion-head-ball-claw-legged coffee table, she always placed a book which illustrated the elegant simplicity of such furniture designers as Marcel Breuer; Eileen Gray; Charles Eames; and American Shakers. Sensei adored her; and loved to hear her relate how, when his father ordered her to give their firstborn son a Chinese name; she secretly asked the clerk to record indelibly the name "Percy" which she mistakenly thought was a very American name. To Sensei, if she had named him Abraham Lincoln Wong, she could not have given him a more Yankee handle.

Preferring the cuisines of Italy and Mexico, Sensei avoided Chinese food and prided himself on not knowing a word of Chinese. He balanced this ignorance by an inability to understand Japanese and, because of its inaccessibility, he did not eat Japanese food.

The Man of Zen who practices Karate obviously is the adventurous type; and Sensei, staying true to type, enjoyed participating in Beryl's and George's investigations. It required little time for him to become a one-third partner of the team. He called himself, "the ampersand in *Wagner & Tilson*."

Sensei Wong may have been better at advertising karate than at performing it, but this merely says that he was a superb huckster for the discipline. In college he had studied civil engineering; but he also was on the fencing team and he regularly practiced gymnastics. He had learned yoga and ancient forms of meditation from his mother. He attained Zen's vaunted transcendental states; which he could access 'on the mat.' It was not surprising that when he began to learn karate he was already half-accomplished. After he won a few minor championships he attracted the attention of several martial arts publications that found his "unprecedented" switchings newsworthy. They imparted to him a "great master" cachet, and perpetuated it to the delight of dojo owners and martial arts shopkeepers. He did win many championships and, through unpaid endorsements and political propaganda, inspired the sale of Japanese weapons, including nunchaku and shuriken which he did not actually use.

Although his Order was strongly given to celibacy, enough wiggle room remained for the priest who found it expedient to marry or dally. Yet, having reached his mid-forties unattached, he regarded it as 'unlikely' that he would ever be romantically welded to a female, and as 'impossible' that he would be bonded to a citizen and custom's agent of the People's Republic of China - whose Gung Fu abilities challenged him and who would strike terror in his heart especially when she wore Manolo Blahnik red spike heels. Such combat, he insisted, was patently unfair, but he prayed that Providence would not level the playing field. He met his femme fatale while working on *A Case of Virga.*

Later in their association Sensei would take under his spiritual wing a young Thai monk who had a degree in computer science and a flair for acting. Akara Chatree, to whom Sensei's master in Taiwan would give the name Shi Yao Xin, loved Shakespeare; but his father - who came from one of Thailand's many noble families - regarded his son's desire to become an actor as we would regard our son's desire to become a hit man. Akara's brothers were all businessmen and professionals; and as the old patriarch lay dying, he exacted a promise from his tall 'matinee-idol' son that he would never tread upon the flooring of a stage. The old man had asked for nothing else, and since he bequeathed a rather large sum of money to his young son, Akara had to content himself with critiquing the performances of actors who were less filially constrained than he. As far as romance is concerned, he had not thought too much about it until he worked on *A Case of Industrial Espionage.* That case took him to Bermuda, and what can a young hero do when he is captivated by a pretty girl who can recite Portia's lines with crystalline insight while lying beside him on a white beach near a blue ocean?

But his story will keep...

WHO IS AKARA CHATREE (SHI QIAN FA)?

It could be argued, and frequently was, that Akara Chatree's solitary personality had been occasioned by his having inherited a considerable amount of money, so much so that less affluent persons - which included all of his associates at the time that he was financially blessed - pestered him so relentlessly to lend them money or to invest in their business ventures, that for the sake of his sanity he was driven to eschew all "friendships." But this would not be true.

It was also suspected that when he realized that the degree of difference between his intelligence and the common man's was many times greater than the difference between the common man's and the ape's, he was forced into a peculiar taxonomic niche, one in which he could "interbreed" socially and sexually with only those individuals who were similarly endowed. This was a ludicrous surmise.

And then it was supposed that he had "taken up the cloth" because he had spiritual ambitions which only the hermit's life could accommodate. Yet, he chose to be a priest rather than a monk, a choice which belied a preference for isolation.

Akara Chatree had simply been purged of the human tendency to assign values to groups of people. He was convinced that beyond saying some five or six billion individuals occupied the earth, no further qualitative descriptions of the psychological sort could be applied. He therefore limited his interactions to specific persons, persons that he could trust and appreciate for their integrity and kindness. He avoided parties, assemblies, and gatherings of any kind that would subject him to the vagaries of strangers.

Bold assertions such as these are not made in the glacial tempo of evolution. They are the stuff of a revolutionary *coup*. All of a man›s channels of opinion must be diverted and directed to engage the turbines of a new uber-view generator, a vantage point that encompasses all universals.

Akara Chatree's revolution occurred when he was fourteen years old. As a child he had casually accepted those class distinctions which served to maintain his family's social position. He was told that the members of his family were judicious and responsible because of their inherent sense of *Noblesse Oblige*. Money, he was assured, had nothing to do with it. Attending private schools in England did not dull the blade of class division.

And then when he was fourteen his "dominion" class made a trip to India to attend a *puja* in Bihar and to tour the state. Akara, the only child of his father's second marriage, expected to meet with four of his half-brothers, sons of his father's first and third marriages. All of Akara's relatives, with the exception of his mother, lived in Thailand, and Bihar was not considered a distant place.

Shortly after the class arrived in India, all three chaperones and half of the student group were stricken with an intestinal disturbance, leaving the hardy half of the young tourists, which included Akara and a school friend, without much in the way of supervision. His half-brothers, however, were chaperoned by a Draconian Theravadin Buddhist uncle.

Told that several pornographic films were going to be shown in a nearby town, Akara, his brothers and his school friend arranged to meet outside the theater. More than familial enjoyment was involved in the reunion. Akara's friend had borrowed money from him to pay a gambling debt which he had not taken seriously until he was beaten senseless by a debt collector. He had not wanted his parents to know the truth of his loss, and so he begged Akara not only to lend him the repayment money but to keep secret its purpose. Akara obliged and asked his older half-brothers if they would lend him five-thousand pounds so that he could pay a personal debt. Akara's friend had promised to give him a substantial part of the repayment when they met at the theater.

As they sneaked away to the town, a late and heavy rain was falling; and just as they assembled, a levee broke and the boys were separated in the ensuing muddy flood. Akara was carried by the current until finally he found himself buried waist-deep in mud from which he could not extricate himself. His school friend heard and acknowledged his cries for help and told his brothers where he was, and then he left. None of them came to help Akara or to direct any of the official rescue personnel to his location.

His brothers had run from the area because they did not want their uncle to learn where they had been and why they had been there. His friend, he realized, had seen a financial opportunity. With Akara dead - as he was sure he would be since so many others in the path of the flood had already perished - he would be relieved of having to repay the debt.

All night, Akara shivered and whimpered, distraught by his abandonment. Towards dawn, a man who cleaned out cesspools for a living began to use his tools to dig a circle around him. The man refused to look in Akara's face or even to speak to him. He simply dug until enough of the thick mud was removed. Then he pulled the exhausted boy out of the morass, put him on a kind of pontoon raft, and poled his way to firm land. He refused to accept money for his efforts, and only after Akara repeatedly asked him his name, did he finally mumble what sounded like "Kyamay Apkimadah."

As he lay Akara on the doorstep of a medical facility, a villager came and hit the man with a broom handle and told Akara to bathe carefully with Ganga River water since his body had made contact with an Untouchable.

It was on that night that Akara Chatree gained his world-view. He did not return to England but instead went directly to Sao Paulo where his mother met him at the airport and took him home to the building that housed her Zen Buddhist Center.

In a room that measured two meters by three meters, he had a bed, a closet, a desk, a lamp, and courtesy of the last man who occupied the room, six books: an English dictionary; the complete works of William Shakespeare; three mathematics books that took him through intermediate and advanced Calculus; and a first year University text in Physics. The bathroom was at the end of the hall. The kitchen was downstairs. Akara went nowhere else for nearly two years — and two hundred books later. When he did emerge from the Center, it was to matriculate at the University. He only agreed to go there because he wanted to master computer science and needed access to the equipment. (Shakespeare he knew and understood far better than any and all members of the English Department.) He had no friends or enemies and he neither carried a cellphone nor accepted visitors at his Zen Center residence. He was pleasant and cooperative, but he said nothing that did not need to be said.

He had one quirk. On the flyleaf of every book he bought from the date beginning with the mudslide, he wrote the name (as he remembered it) of the man who had helped him. Kyamay Apkimadah

Akara was twenty-three years old and working on his PhD in Computer Science before he learned from a Sanskrit professor that no doubt the words that had been spoken to him were not anyone's name, but simple Hindi for "I help you."

Kyā maiṁ āpakī madada. क्या मैं आपकी मदद.

That night, in 2007, Akara Chatree cried for several hours and then asked his mother to prepare him to take Holy Orders. He became the Zen Buddhist priest, Shi Qian Fa of the Yun Men (Ummon) lineage.

In China he mentioned to his master that he did not want to join the clerical staff of a large business-like temple. He was therefore directed to the little Zen temple on Germantown Avenue, in Philadelphia, and in 2012 he became an assistant to his master's old friend, Sensei Percy Wong (Shi Yao Feng). He moved into the second floor of the temple along with his sixteen server cluster of computer "stuff." He also rented a garage nearby so that he could park his new bright red Corvette inside it.

Eventually, he obtained his private investigator's license. The first case he worked on was The Case of the Insurance Fraud Sacrifices; The Thorn Crown Murder is the second case.

MONDAY, JUNE 3, 2013

It is a peculiar quirk of human nature that someone who has not attained the pinnacle of spiritual ascendance is infinitely more persuasive about having attained it than someone who actually has. The one who has will likely sigh and, seeing the futility of trying to describe the ineffable, will keep silent or humbly repeat Michelangelo's near-death comment: *Ancora imparo.* (I am still learning.) The one who hasn't often displays the "confidence of completion" that is so wondrously attractive. To his followers, the unaccomplished claimant will supply a splendid account of his summit tour as he describes in detail the features of what is yet to him *terra incognito.*

Those narrators who have an egotistical or a pecuniary motive may do considerable harm, particularly to the gullible who have check books; but when we exclude from consideration those who are deceitful, we are left with the would-be "Nirvana tourists" who are harmlessly ingenuous. They truly believe that they have reached the goal; and for so long as their hearts are pure, they alone will suffer for the error. This will come when they encounter the stage that lies between the altitude that they *have* attained and the top.

Sensei had made such an error. He had encountered that intervening stage, and he was suffering.

Ostensibly, on this Monday morning, he was trying to compose the evening's Dharma talk as he sat alone at the front desk of the offices of Wagner & Tilson, Private Investigators, "minding the store" while his associate detectives were out of the office, working on cases. He had been sitting there for two hours, and his pen had not moved.

It occurred to him that everything he had ever taught was inconsequential and that the subject that was of the greatest significance to mankind was one that he did not even understand.

Yes. Yes. Sensei Percy Wong had given his sangha Zen's standard homilies on every man's need to become independent, to extricate himself from adolescent entanglements and entertainments, to cease making arbitrary judgments about those who are his friends and will always have his back even as they give him the shirt off theirs, and those who are his enemies and are therefore sub-human and needful of being disturbed or destroyed. He had repeatedly warned his congregation that aside from usually being wrong in these assumptions, the habit of making such judgments predisposed a man to seek his self-image in the eyes of other people, whereas the ego's battle for detached maturity could be won only when a man sought his image in the eyes of his interior Buddha Self.

He had preached that to become a Man of Zen it was necessary to follow the Buddha's dictum: "One man may conquer ten thousand men in battle, and another man may conquer only himself; but this man is the greater victor."

Sensei practiced what he preached and assumed that once a man achieved a warrior's self-discipline, perhaps even with that Samurai aplomb that is bound tightly by a Black Belt, he would attain an internal calmness and would respond to turmoil, "Like a clock that continues to tick steadily in the midst of a thunderstorm."

He knew, theoretically at least, that until a man ceased to be obsessed with parents, siblings, friends, and enemies, he could not commit himself to any enduring relationship and become a successful husband and father. The immature man would remain, despite vows made at marriage altars, a victim of his own adolescent self-interest.

Sensei took the result of self-mastery for granted, and he went on with a pure, albeit naive, heart to distinguish himself in Kyudo, the Japanese long bow and arrow - the *yumi* and *ya*. He had politely laughed when his turn came to compete against Cupid. And then he was felled by the little fellow's first arrow and found himself permanently wounded and defenseless.

And so it happened that in his 42nd year to heaven, Sensei met a customs agent from Hong Kong, Miss Sonya Lee, and he fell in love and discovered that nothing else in his life mattered to him in quite the way that she did. *And he had not heard from her in months.*

It was not possible, he knew, that she had replaced him with another man. But it was possible - since she did have a dangerous occupation - that she was dead, or being held captive, or lying helpless and injured in some jungle outpost, or in any place that she could not reach him to let him know that she was still alive, and still *his* Sonya, and still waiting for him to come and save her.

And so he sat there, stymied in the attempt to write a simple Dharma talk because he could not think. His mind oscillated between the poles of blankness and riotous confusion and did not stop at any place long enough to form a thought worth recording. He was miserable in the limbo of waiting for news about the one and only love of his life, and he was a beginner in that affair of the heart in which one cares for someone else more than one cares for oneself. In short, Love had come late to Sensei Wong, and he did not understand that its agonies could be meted out to the same degree as its ecstasies. His internal clock had quit ticking.

When his fears for Sonya became too much to bear, he would employ a Zen technique and expel the worrisome thoughts from his mind, and then he would sit, staring blankly at the desk, or at the street scene, or at the same unmarked page of a notepad on which he was supposed to be writing.

He prayed that in the terrible hours of waiting he would be given something that would ease the sharpness of his pain and the infernal dullness of his mind.

And then, as if in answer to his prayer, the office door opened and an elderly man dressed in khaki fatigues and carrying a book that looked suspiciously like a Bible entered the room.

Sensei, dressed in ordinary street clothing, dreaded the possibility that he was going to be preached to. "Can I help you?" he weakly asked.

"Would you be averse to helping a fugitive?" the man answered, advancing toward him.

Sensei's heart sank. It was too late to claim that he did not speak English. He braced himself. "From where?" he asked.

"Mozambique," the man answered.

Sensei sat up. He was not prepared to hear the name of a place that could be located on a Google map. "You're wanted in Mozambique? For what?"

"No. I'm not here for myself. My nephew is the fugitive, and he needs professional help. He can't go to Mozambique himself to find proof that he's innocent."

"I guess not. If he's a fugitive, his guilt is pretty much decided. Why don't you sit down and tell me about it? What crime was he charged with?"

As the man sat down he placed his book, which Sensei now saw was a text on big game hunting, on the desk. "He's been accused of murdering his father."

Sensei introduced himself, enthusiastically half-standing to reach across the desk to shake hands with his visitor who said, in a bewildered voice, "I'm Charles Thompson. My brother is, or rather was, Devers Thompson. He made a fortune in pharmaceuticals." He paused to clear his throat and to allow Sensei to sit down and take the pose of an interested listener. "Devers left two sons: Gordon who's twenty-four - he's the fugitive - and Jackson who's twenty-two. They are the heirs to his considerable estate. I'm the unlucky fellow who agreed to be the trustee-executor."

"A murder charge would make your job a little awkward," Sensei noted. "Tell me how all this trouble came about."

"My brother Devers was an adventurer, a sailor, an explorer. He also loved to hunt and has a den, or 'man cave' as he jokingly referred to it, filled with the stuffed heads of trophy animals. But some years ago he accidentally stepped into an animal trap and damaged his foot so badly that he couldn't stroll through a park let alone trek through a jungle or savannah. He could still sail though, so he refitted his three-masted schooner, *The Patent Pirate,* and planned to take a trip with his sons.

"Devers wanted them to experience an ocean voyage under sail and the thrill of big game hunting and fishing. They would sail The Patent

Pirate across the Atlantic, up the east coast of Africa to Mozambique, and while Gordon stayed with my brother to go fishing, Jackson would go on a lion safari in Mozambique, one of the few places left where it is legal to hunt a wild male cat in the wild.

"Jackson was excited and bought himself a new Browning .375 rifle and a jungle wardrobe. Jackson tended to lack confidence in himself, and Devers thought the hunt would bring out the macho in him. My brother also had a Browning .375. It was one of his favorite guns. Since he was no longer capable of hunting, he gave the rifle to Gordon who kept it in his cabin for protection.

"They dropped anchor at a mooring outside the city of Beira which is at the delta of the Pungue River.

"At dawn of September 3rd, a crewman took Jackson to shore where he met his safari agency's guide. That same day, Gordon and my brother leased a small cabin cruiser and went out to fish. Gordon joked and said they were after coelacanth which live in those waters. He said he'd stuff the fish and hang it over the fireplace and that it would be more interesting than a lion's head, which is probably true."

Sensei laughed, and Thompson paused to acknowledge the humor of hunting the rare and ancient fish.

"It started to rain after Gordon and my brother had gone out less than a mile," he continued, "so they turned back. The ship's crew had gone ashore and only one man, Tod Beckridge, Jackson's best friend from college, was on board when they returned–"

Sensei interrupted him. "Are you saying that Jackson brought his best friend along for the transatlantic voyage but didn't take him on the main adventure - the safari? That doesn't register somehow. Why didn't Tod go hunting, too?"

"A genuine lion hunt costs a minimum of $35,000. Tod's family once had money, but they lost it in some bad investments. Tod had to work his way through college. Devers admired the boy's work-ethic and offered to pay for him, but Tod declined, saying he'd go another time.

"Gordon had brought DVDs with him and says he went to his cabin to watch movies. He didn't see his father all afternoon. He missed him at dinner and inquired after him, but no one had seen him. The rented cabin cruiser was still at the dock. Gordon didn't know what to think. Tod told him that in the morning, before they went fishing, he had overheard Devers talking to someone about having a few drinks on shore later in the day.

"At dawn of the following morning, September 4th, a fisherman found Devers' body floating in the ocean half-way to Madagascar. He had been shot. The slug was identified as a .375 Winchester. The Browning that Gordon kept on The Patent Pirate was missing.

"Tod, the one person who was aboard when they returned from the fishing trip, claimed that he hadn't actually seen Devers since the morning of the 3rd, but he had heard Devers and Gordon arguing early in the day. Gordon insisted that no such argument ever occurred and that maybe he mistook the sounds of a film he was watching. Tod had assumed the argument had occurred before they left on the cabin cruiser, but he couldn't be sure.

"The will stipulates that if one of the sons died or was otherwise unable to inherit by virtue of permanent mental defect or some similar impediment, physical or moral, the other son, at my discretion, could reap the benefit of his inheritance. There was a provision, naturally, for any medical care needed by one who didn't inherit. Needless to say, if Gordon is convicted of killing his father, he is automatically disqualified. Jackson will get his own half, and I will oversee the distribution of Gordon's half."

Charles Thompson paused in his narrative, and Sensei, assuming that he was to fill the interim with a substantive comment, could only manage, "Hmm. I see."

"The authorities believed that the argument Tod overheard between Gordon and his father was the motive; the missing rifle was the means, and the fishing trip was the opportunity. They devised a scenario, created from the minus 45 degree angle at which the bullet was fired into Devers' chest: Gordon had pushed his father overboard and shot him, leaving him to die as he then tossed the rifle in the water and brought the boat back to shore."

"That's a large bullet," Sensei noted. "Wouldn't it have passed right through him at such close range?"

"My brother was a big man... over three hundred pounds. Maybe Devers was underwater when he was shot. Maybe the gunpowder had deteriorated from age or improper storage. I obtained forensic photographs of the slug they removed from my brother's chest."

"What did you hope to learn from the photographs?" Sensei asked.

"I wanted to be sure that it hadn't come from Jackson's rifle. While I don't believe either boy capable of such an act, I thought that of the two brothers, Jackson was more likely to be guilty. He had been in serious drug and gambling trouble. Two thugs had been trying to collect debts. They pursued him - which is another reason my brother took the boys on the trip. Gordon was quiet and studious, with no detectable vices. But Jackson was another story.

"When Jackson finally received word, he returned to the yacht on September 6th, carrying the iced head of a 350 pound lion which he immediately air-freighted to Italy. That's where it would begin the many months of freeze-dry processing. A taxidermist in Mozambique's Manica Province had been hired to decapitate the beast. In the rush to get back, Jackson's new Browning rifle was also lost or stolen.

"A fisherman claimed to have seen Devers return to shore with Gordon, but no one would believe him since he had a reputation for lying. Another longshoreman told the first mate that he had heard a rumor that Jackson had killed his lion in what is called 'a canned hunt,' and he therefore had plenty of time to go back and forth to Beira. It was only some 80 or 90 miles between the safari area and the place the ship was moored."

"A 'canned hunt'?" Sensei asked. "Isn't that when the quarry is a captive animal that's let loose in some kind of fenced enclosure?"

"Yes. Most of the time spent on a genuine hunt is spent locating and then stalking the wild animal. In a canned hunt, you can drive to the area, pay the money, and shoot the half-tamed prey in fifteen minutes. These activities are banned in Mozambique."

"I see. Please go on," Sensei said.

"Inquiries were made and it was determined that Jackson hadn't participated in any 'canned hunt.' The longshoreman and the fisherman, miffed, I suppose, because they weren't believed, secretly helped Gordon to escape.

"With both sons aboard, The Patent Pirate was soon rounding the Cape of Good Hope and heading home."

"If your purpose is to have us investigate the murder of Devers Thompson," Sensei said, "I think I ought to advise you that it will be an expensive undertaking. We'd send two operatives on such an assignment, and one of them would have to be George Wagner, who is the most experienced of our group."

"Money is no problem. I've got plenty of my own. As it is, your fee will come out of the estate that's valued at $90 million. I can't settle the inheritance until the problem is resolved. I want the rumors put to rest. All of them. I can't bear to think that either boy is a killer. I also want to know who really did kill my brother! So you can charge whatever you like."

Sensei googled a map of Mozambique. "I see that Manica Province is inland."

"Yes. Jackson's rifle may still be there. You can identify it by the 'JT' carved into the base of the stock. If someone should claim ownership of the gun, I ask only for a slug fired from it so that the rifling can be compared to the slug taken from my brother's body."

"You could confirm that it was the same rifle or a different rifle, but you still wouldn't know who pulled the trigger. You said that Jackson's rifle was lost or stolen..."

"If it turned out to be Jackson's rifle, I'd be paying you to determine where he was between noon and 3 p.m. of September 3rd, the medical examiner's estimation of the time of death, and also, naturally, to at least try to discover who did kill my brother."

"Did Devers have any other enemies or people there who would have benefited from his death?"

"None. I'd have known. The crew liked him. He admired Tod and regarded him as a good influence on Jackson. Tod was Jackson's best friend since they were in kindergarden.

"Ah, yes. I'm included. In the event you need to know my whereabouts at the time of the crime, I'm a scout master with my church and was in the Pocono Mountains with several troops from August 25th until September 8th. I was out of phone reach and didn't learn about my brother's death until Jackson and Gordon called me on September 6th. Gordon was arrested on the 8th. He escaped on September 10th. There was nothing for me to do but to wait until The Patent Pirate crossed the Atlantic. They didn't get back until November. Would you be one of the two detectives who investigate?" Thompson asked.

"No," Sensei said. "The case doesn't sound like a short one and, to be honest, I'm a Zen Buddhist priest. My ministry is down the street in that little Zen temple near the corner. I also have a P.I. license - George Wagner and Beryl Tilson, the principal investigators of this agency, are members of my congregation. I got in the habit of helping them out on cases so I just went ahead and made it official."

"Do you have any qualms about killing animals... especially for sport? I ask because I wouldn't want to prejudice further Jackson's position in this calamity. Aren't all you folks vegetarians... opposed to killing animals?"

"No. Some are, and some aren't. Some of the strictest Buddhists who live on islands consider only mammals to be animals. They regard themselves as non-violent vegetarians, but they do eat fish, shrimp, crabs, and other seafood. Regardless of definitions, we can't deny the Dharma to people who live in the Arctic or places in which they can't grow vegetables. They have to kill animals for food.

"But when you're considering big game hunting, you have a legitimate concern. Killing for the entertainment of it is abhorrent; on the other hand, the serious hunter can perform a service as well as achieve a spiritual experience that is as profound as it is esoteric. Without getting into that aspect of it, we should consider the number of folks who earn an honest living from the activity, and also how killing rogue male lions, for example, isn't such a bad thing. They're the ones who kill people and livestock."

Thompson understood. "Yes, and they also kill a third of the lion cubs a pride produces. As far as the big-game safari business is concerned, the country is managing it responsibly."

"Is Gordon considered a wanted man in the U.S.?" Sensei asked.

"Mozambique," Thompson explained, "has no extradition treaty with us. Gordon is temporarily beyond their reach, although I understand that negotiations for his return are underway. They want him to be brought back to stand trial particularly because of the escape. So there is a time element. I'd like you to get started with this as soon as possible."

"Why did it take so long for you to seek help?"

"We were under the impression that the authorities in Maputo, the capital, decided that there was insufficient evidence to pursue the trial; but then they changed their mind. Apparently they had received a copy of my brother's will which had been translated into their official language, Portuguese. They then formally expressed a desire to try him."

"Let me call George Wagner. I'll get an answer for you immediately." Sensei called George and outlined the assignment. "Akara would be eager to go," he said.

George, too, was eager for some excitement. "Is he definitely willing to go?"

"I think he'd quit if we didn't ask him," Sensei answered. "Ever since he got his P.I. license he's been itching for a big job. This could be it."

"If Thompson's willing to pay business class airfare and $20K for me and $15K for Akara, we'll take the assignment. Any funds not spent will be returned. If we run out of money, he'll have to pay more. You can never tell about bribes that need to be paid. Get him to sign the contract and then get Akara to sit in when you ask all the relevant backstory questions. Make the plane reservations for next week. I'll be home tonight. But remember... if Akara doesn't want to go, you're elected."

Sensei explained the terms and Charles Thompson signed the contract and wrote a check for $35,000. Sensei called Akara Chatree at the temple and asked him to walk down to the investigators' office for the interview.

As soon as Akara agreed to the assignment, Thompson made flight and hotel reservations for the following week. They would need to obtain online visas and get malaria and yellow fever shots.

Akara asked, "Where is the lion's head at this time?"

"At my brother's residence in Media. It only recently arrived from Italy."

"And the two brothers?"

"Jackson and Gordon both live in the house with me. Ah!" he said, remembering something important. "On Saturday night Jackson is giving a party to debut the head. Why don't you come as my guests, and you can meet them and see the lion? It's hanging in the den."

"For the party," Akara asked, "will the attire be formal?"

"Yes. Jackson's a bit of a snob."

Sensei silently groaned. George would not be happy to hear that he'd have to wear evening clothes and sit in the passenger's seat of Akara's Corvette.

"Fathers, sons, brothers, and friends," Sensei muttered to himself, "can make for one messy mix." He locked the office and returned to the temple.

A voicemail message was waiting for him. Father Willem DeVries had called and wanted a call back as soon as possible. He had "a little" information about the whereabouts of Sonya Lee.

DeVries had a friend who worked for Interpol. At Christmas he had offered to ask his friend to help locate Sonya, but Sensei declined, reasonably fearing that if she were working undercover, calling attention to the whereabouts of a beautiful Chinese woman of her intelligence and knowledge of smuggling was not the smartest thing that someone who loved her could do. He decided to be more patient. By Easter, however, his patience was exhausted. Desperate, he did not decline when deVries again asked him if he should call his friend at Interpol. Two months had passed and now, finally, there was "a little" information.

Sensei's hands were clammy, and his mouth was so dry that his lips stuck to his teeth. He returned the call.

DeVries did not waste time on pleasantries. "My friend from Interpol just called to tell me that in a ship's explosion off the coast of Attu in the Aleutian Islands, last October, Sonya Lee was critically injured. He had no other details. He says he'll continue to search. He's trying to find the hospital she was taken to. Oh... she was retired from Hong Kong Customs. It may take a few more days so he says to be patient and not to interfere. You will compromise his contacts."

Sensei stood motionless, holding onto the receiver of the kitchen wall-phone, but he did not really understand what deVries was saying. "Could you go over that again?" he asked. Akara Chatree came into the kitchen.

By the time Willem deVries repeated the message, Sensei had begun to shake. His knees buckled and he tried to sit on a chair but succeeded only in sending the chair scraping across the tile floor as he stumbled and fell. Akara helped him to his feet. "Let me make you some tea. It will calm you."

Sensei looked up at him and said, "What?"

"I'll make you some tea," Akara repeated. "It will calm you." He helped Sensei to sit at the table.

The months of agony - the information black-out at her office, the incessant worrying that Sonya was dead or captured or being tortured while all the while he was hoping that he hadn't heard from her because she could not break her cover by contacting him - all the speculation had stopped. An explosion could mean burns and injuries of extreme violence. Hers were severe enough to end her career. He felt a specific fear. The months of anxious possibilities had been torn away from his mind like the pages of a day calendar. A flurry of them, like leaves that were sere and ready to fall, had all suddenly been blown out of his brain, and he sat at the kitchen table, unable to see anything but a blur of white that swirled around him.

Finally, he put his head down on the table and began to chant the Heart Sutra.

SATURDAY, JUNE 8, 2013

"Look!" Beryl said as she buckled George's cummerbund in the back. "Your diet has paid off. I'm no longer trying to fit a chihuahua's collar on a shar pei. Aren't you glad I nagged you into shape? You look like Cary Grant."

"He's dead."

She tugged on the buckle. "You're not breathing, either. You can stop holding your breath. The diet didn't work that big a miracle."

George relaxed. "Don't close the lid just yet. I feel a pulse." He checked to see that the pleats in the cummerbund were pointed up in the correct direction for non-military use. "It's a little snug but at least it fits. Yes, I'm almost back to where I was twenty-two years ago as a college grad. I still fit in the same patent leather pumps. We're not getting enough money for this assignment. I should have charged him twenty G's just to put on this penguin suit. Fix my tie and keep your comments to yourself."

"It isn't that I don't enjoy being your valet, but with Sensei a nervous wreck and you and Akara getting ready to fly off to Africa, I'm starting to wonder how long I'll have to be in charge of both the temple and the office - not to mention keeping your house plants watered. Where is Sensei now?" Beryl asked.

"At the temple. I told him to close up shop at 5 p.m. and go back to the temple. He can fake his way through tomorrow's Dharma talk. Check up on him when you get back. With Akara on his way here to get me, Sensei's all alone. If he should get bad news about Sonya I want you to call me. Akara and I will leave the party immediately."

She finished tying the bow. "Be sure you take lots of selfies with that lion's head. You and your alter-ego Leo! Two guys with great hair."

George laughed. "He's hung on the wall."

"Stand on a chair."

The doorbell rang. "If you say," George said, "'Your date is here,' I will toss you out the window."

Beryl ran down the steps. "Akara!" she called. "Your date is running a little late."

Akara Chatree, as tall as George but twenty pounds lighter, cut a Byronesque figure as they entered the Thompsons' home. They were not fashionably late. George wanted to interview the two brothers, and he did not want them to be drunk when he questioned them.

Gordon Thompson, the first to greet them, gave the appearance of being studious - not of an academic subject, but rather of himself. He seemed hesitant to reveal anything personal for fear, perhaps, that he would not understand the subject sufficiently to respond to questions. He therefore was wary, guarded, and as poised to depart from the conversation as a bee that had selected a barren flower to light on. He was tall, slim, clear-eyed, and attractive in appearance. He introduced himself and then said, "I don't believe I've had the pleasure..."

It was clear that Charles Thompson had not informed him that he had invited the private investigators to the party or even that he had engaged their services. Ordinarily it would have irritated George to have to explain that they were working on his behalf, but there was something likable about Gordon. George simply said, "Your Uncle Charles has engaged me and my colleague, Dr. Chatree, to prove your innocence of the crime of–"

"–Patricide, I believe it's called." Gordon smiled as if to indicate the charge's implausibility. "You're going to Mozambique?" he asked quizzically.

"Next Monday," George replied. "We'd like to ask you a few questions in private."

"Follow me into the library... please." Gordon gestured and led the way to the other side of the huge house.

They went to the corner of the book-filled room and sat on overstuffed leather chairs. "I'm finding the pair of you to be reminiscent of Holmes and Watson. Sleuth and physician. I hope your solution to my problem comes as inevitably."

"My degree," Akara said, affecting regret, "is in computer science, not medicine."

"Even better, these days," Gordon replied, picking up a decanter and indicating that they might enjoy some scotch whiskey.

George put his palm up. "We're working, but thanks for the offer."

Gordon replaced the bottle and asked, "What did you want to know?"

"First, what is your relationship to Tod Beckridge?" George asked.

"He's my brother's friend. Jackson also dates Tod's sister, Norma."

"When we go back to the party, point them out to us. Have you any idea how or why your father left the ship on the day you aborted your fishing trip?"

"I heard nothing. But I was watching movies. Because quarters are cramped on a ship, I use earphones to get the sound."

"But wait a minute... Tod said that he overheard an argument and that you assumed it was a movie you were playing."

"I couldn't call him a liar since, frankly, I didn't know whose argument he could have overheard. The deckhands could have been arguing. And a couple of times the earphones did get a little uncomfortable so I listened without them. But a laptop's speakers are not all that powerful. I didn't know what he heard. I definitely did not argue with my dad."

"Are you convinced that your brother was in Manica Province when your dad was killed?"

"He did bag a lion. It's hanging on the wall of the den right now."

"All that you know, Gordon, is that there is a lion's head hanging on the wall of the den. Who killed the lion is what we have to prove. Your brother is still a prime suspect."

"Jackson? I admit I first thought that he could be responsible, but I had to rule that out. I found out that he did, in fact, kill the lion on

September 3rd. He took it to a taxidermist on that date." He continued speaking in a tone usually used by those who are quoting scripture. "He was trying to recover his lost rifle which is the reason we couldn't reach him immediately."

George sighed. "Gordon, I don't like to deal with naive people. If you're engaged to find a thief and you tell a naive person that it is his friend who is stealing from him, he goes and tells his friend that you said he's stealing from him. How can you rule him out especially when there's a possibility that Tod was an accomplice?"

"I'm not naive. My mother died ten years ago and my father was murdered less than a year ago. My brother and I are all that's left of my immediate family, and I don't look forward to finding out that not only did my brother kill my father, but that he tried to have me blamed for it. I'm not stupid. He's the one who'd benefit most. Yes, Tod Beckridge very probably lied for him about that argument. Norma Beckridge wouldn't mind at all spending my half of the inheritance, which Jackson might get if I'm convicted or otherwise found unqualified to inherit my half of the estate. I did some checking on my own. He was in Manica province on the 3rd. He did come home with the lion. And Tod is nobody's dupe. He's independent and, as they say, 'made of sterner stuff.'"

"Your father was fond of Tod. Any chance that Tod could have gotten him to go fishing later, when you were watching movies?"

"No. I dismissed any thought about that, too. My dad was not all that keen about going fishing in the first place. He had gained a lot of weight after his foot injury, and climbing up and down from one ship to get into another was difficult for him. He couldn't put his weight fully on his damaged foot. Worse, it's necessary to brace yourself with your feet when you're reeling in large game fish. He sat in one of the two special fishing chairs in the stern and worried that if he did get something on the line he'd either lose the rod or get pulled overboard. They had a harness but he was too fat for it. Also, he didn't like the fumes from the exhaust."

"Doesn't your schooner have a life boat? Could Tod and your father have decided to use that boat to fish for smaller fish and avoid the fumes and the harness?"

"Our dinghy has a detachable outboard motor, but it has oars, too. It's a small craft and sitting on a flat board inside it would not be a 350 pound man's idea of a pleasant afternoon of ocean fishing."

"But if you checked up on Jackson, you must have thought it possible that he returned to the ship and asked your father to go out with him."

"Yes. And probably if he had come back saying that he was afraid to go into the bush but didn't want the trip to be a total loss... that maybe he could catch a big game fish... my dad would have gone. Sooner than make Jackson feel like a coward, he would have gone. But I determined that Jackson did kill a lion on the day he left. He didn't have to come back in some kind of sportsman's disgrace."

"You verified that on the day of the murder Jackson was only eighty miles away and in possession of a dead lion. There's train and road and air transportation available. And you still don't know who shot the lion. How's your brother's attitude been towards you and the trial? Do you suspect him of being behind the government's change of heart in wanting to stand trial? Someone sent them a copy of the will."

Gordon Thompson did not want to answer. He got up and walked to the window. "That's been a big source of worry for me," he said. "I..." A gust of wind suddenly blew, and an outdoor light illuminated time-loosened jasmine flowers that silently struck the window panes like bits of tissue paper. He waited until the gust subsided and then continued, "I haven't asked him about it, but I still don't know why they changed their mind."

"Is there a copy of the will lying around?" George asked.

"Yes," Gordon said, opening a desk drawer. "Here it is." He brought it to George.

George looked at it and noticed in one of the final paragraphs just how much of the disposition of the assets was left to the discretion of Charles Thompson. He handed the document to Akara. "With your permission," he said to Gordon, "I'd like to have my associate check around with all the translation services to see if anyone officially translated this document into Portuguese."

"Portuguese?" Gordon asked.

"Yes. Didn't you know that it was upon receipt of an official Portuguese translation of the will that the government decided to pursue the case more vigorously?"

Gordon sighed. "No. I didn't know. I can save you the trouble. I saw a charge on our house-expense credit card... it was from ProForma Translation in Upper Darby for $1400 a few months ago. I asked Jackson about it and was told it was about a shipping charge for the Italian company that freeze-dried the lion's head. I had a hard time accepting that story. Why would translating a bill of lading cost $1400? But check with them. If it is Portuguese then it was Jackson who sent them a copy and probably suggested that the motive was an inheritance of millions." He furled his eyebrows over closed eyes and appeared to be genuinely distressed.

Akara nodded. "It's a poor country. More than one civil servant could see benefit in levying big fines against you. Maybe that's all they're really after. You escaped. Trying to regain custody of you was probably expensive." He got out a slim tablet in his tuxedo jacket and made a note. "Incidentally, since your uncle has so much discretion in distributing your funds, we ran a credit check on him. He certainly doesn't need money."

"That's why my father trusted him. He had even more money than my father. He's a widower who married very well, and he doesn't have any kids."

"We've heard about Jackson's drug and gambling troubles, but do either of you have any serious problems? Psychological? Genetic? Any other addictions? Cult memberships? Any Lady MacBeth type of ambitious or greedy women in your lives?"

Gordon sighed. "We thought at one time that Jackson had schizophrenia. He had begun to act strangely. It turned out that he was playing what the kids at his school called 'Pill Roulette.' They would put pills in a jar and, blindfolded, reach in and take a few of them. They never knew what they had swallowed. They would take videos of their actions. Most of the pills came from their parents' prescriptions so there were no charges brought."

"That was kid-experimentation," George said. "What about when he was older?"

"My father once found a crack pipe in his bedroom. He didn't know what it was and Jackson told him it was for an Indian weed the girls smoked. He said they liked it because it helped them to dull their appetite and lose weight. I don't think my dad believed him."

"Does he still have any drug debts?"

"I don't know. My mother left each of us close to a million dollars worth of bearer bonds that we got when we turned twenty-one. I invested mine. I don't know what he did with his. I've suspected all along that he owed money to unsavory people, possibly drug dealers... maybe gamblers. He goes to Atlantic City frequently. A couple of grubby guys - tough types - once came to the house looking for Jackson. That's what prompted my father to refit the schooner and take us on vacation last year."

"One last question," George said. "Usually a big game hunter has at least two rifles. We know only of the Browning .375 that he left with. Did he have another rifle?"

"No, not with him. He intended to rent a second weapon."

They returned to the party. Gordon led them to Charles Thompson who introduced them to Jackson as his friends, making no mention of their being private investigators.

Jackson, who looked remarkably like his brother, extended his hand and muttered a perfunctory greeting while he simultaneously signaled to someone who had had just entered the room. Without looking at George or Akara a second time, he flitted across the room, leaving them to look at each other and laugh. "He's high," Akara said, "and he wants people to believe that his excitement is due to their presence. His eyeballs and his fingers are dancing."

"But not with each other," George concurred, laughing. "I expect him to start singing show tunes. If we question him, we might induce the performance." His attention turned to a red-haired young woman who was staring at Akara. "Don't look now," George said, "but that pretty gal over there is giving you a look that's got more messages in it than a microwave tower."

Akara could not resist turning to see his admirer. She was tall, and the cream silk sheath she wore gave her an obelisk's exclamation point of notice as she stood in front of a darkly paneled wall. A fillet of large diamonds crossed her forehead and disappeared into her hair's ornately coiffed braids and curls. Akara remembered the Breck ads his roommate had framed as posters in their dorm room. She looked like one of them, and he thought that she was one of the most beautiful women he had ever seen. Not until another woman who was heavily made up approached her and "air-kissed" her cheeks, did he realize that she was not wearing any make-up at all. "How do you know that she's looking at me? She could just as easily be looking at you," he whispered.

"No," George countered, "she's like a shark that can identify the blood of net worth in the water." The line made Akara smile and he nodded at her as George added, "She also can probably sense the sexual performance that accompanies the testosterone of youth. Go with God, little brother."

Akara knew his net worth, and his tailor had assured him that he wore his garments very well. But the idea of "sexual performance" amused him. He tended not to regard a sexual encounter as a soliloquy that could be separated from the rest of the drama. Intimacy with strangers was a contradiction in terms. "I think she's giving me one of those 'come hither' smiles," he whispered. "Excuse me," he said to George and proceeded to walk across the room to greet her.

Akara was not surprised to learn that she was Norma Beckridge and that the stoic young man in steel rimmed glasses who stood beside her was her brother Tod.

Norma seemed, at first, to have the same aloof and untouchable demeanor that characterized Tod. More, Akara thought, since she seemed to be acting as though she were the hostess, the alpha female of the assembled group. She signaled a waiter with only a slight wave of her hand, which indicated to the young priest that the waiter must have been watching her for instructions.

As Akara approached and nodded, she said, "Norma Beckridge," using the same crisp delivery that might have prefaced the words, "for the defense," and, gesturing with an upturned palm, added, "this is my brother Tod." Akara smiled, more to himself than to them. He was thinking, "And this is my second chair Tod." Akara introduced himself as a friend of Charles.

The waiter brought a tray of flute-shaped champagne glasses. An awkward moment followed. None of the three cared to take a glass. The waiter bowed and walked away.

"And I suppose," Akara said to the imperious red-head, "your relationship to Jackson makes you the designated hostess."

"Only in a manner of speaking," she said cryptically. "But yes, Charles is a widower, Devers is dead, Gordon is a solitary man, and Jackson's been my - shall we say - escort for the last few years. If that's what it takes to be considered the group's alpha-female, I suppose I'm it. Are you in business, Mr. Chatree?"

"Only indirectly," he said. "I'm a Zen Buddhist priest... out of uniform, as you can see."

"In a celibate order?" Tod asked.

"No, not celibate... just conservative."

Tod noticed someone across the room. He raised his hand in greeting and excused himself, leaving Akara alone with Norma.

Akara looked at George for help but Gordon Thompson had engaged George in conversation and was now blocking Akara's line of view. His own predicament made him want to laugh. He asked himself, "What would George do? WWGD?" The bemused expression that formed itself on his face seemed to intrigue Norma. Akara touched her elbow and gestured at several portraits. "Would you care to identify some of these people for me?"

They walked together along a gallery of paintings, stopping only when they came to a portrait of a handsome man wearing a hunter's bush fatigues. "Devers Thompson," Norma said, wistfully. "He cut quite a figure." She sighed. "I lost my virginity to him ten years ago... right around the time this portrait was painted. He gained a hundred fifty pounds after that."

Akara did not know how to respond. It was at moments like this, he realized, that he did not know much about women. "That was before he had the trap accident?" he asked.

"Yes. He taught me to ride, to hunt, to sail and, above all, to appreciate beautiful things."

"Like diamonds?"

"Obviously. Diamonds are the most beautiful things in the world."

Again, Akara could find no suitable follow-up to a statement that he had never before heard in his life. "What was he like after the accident?"

"A hog with his foot always elevated in a plaster cast. He kept his legs apart to prevent his genitals from getting," she looked at him with mock severity, "prickly heat - no pun intended. It always made me think of a lame dog trying to urinate. And then the belly fat started to form into an enormous sack of guts that rolled right over his penis. His breasts were 'Double D,' I swear. If one stranger were to ask another stranger, 'What is the gender of that creature?' the answer would be a guess."

Again, Akara did not know how to respond. He smiled and let his hand graze the hollow of her back. "Let's join the others and see the famous lion," he whispered in a tone that he hoped sounded sexy.

In the den they saw not only the mounted lion's head but also, on an easel, a blow-up of the obligatory photograph of Jackson kneeling beside the whole dead lion while holding the Browning Safari rifle. George approached them and after all the introductions were made, took a series of photographs of the trophy, alone and with the case principals, and the photo blow-up of Jackson and the missing Browning. At Norma's insistence he took several photos of her and Akara. Akara looked around and saw that Tod Beckridge was looking at him and Norma with a strange, almost jealous look on his face.

At the sound of thunder, Norma murmured, "We're going to have some rain." Then a tapping sound on the windows made her update the weather forecast. "No, it's raining now. What a shame! All the silk shoes will be ruined."

George nudged Akara. "I'm afraid that we need to leave the party. I have another commitment." She extended her hand, and George took it in his left hand and bent over and kissed her knuckles. "Wonderful perfume," he said. "I'll remember it for a long time."

There was another clap of thunder. "Well, good night," Akara said. When Norma extended her hand to him, he shook it. "It's been a pleasure," he said.

She reached into a small clutch purse she was carrying and withdrew a calling card. "My number's on the back. Call me. Perhaps we can do lunch." She slid the card into his breast pocket. "You can't walk to your car in the rain. I won't hear of it." She raised her hand again and with a slight flick, summoned a young waiter. "Bring Mr. Chatree's car around to the portico." The waiter put his palm out waiting to receive the keys.

Gordon Thompson corrected her. "It's Doctor Chatree."

Akara smiled politely. "Can you drive a manual transmission?" he asked the waiter.

"No. I never learned."

"Then we'll just have to get a little wet," George said, nudging Akara again. "We arrived early," he explained. "We're parked close to the house."

They were the first to leave the party. Norma Beckridge stood on the portico and waved as George and Akara got into the Corvette.

As they drove back to town, George noted, "Drugs and gambling have added bigger elements of danger than what we'd find on a safari. Use your computer stuff to find out whatever you can about Jackson's history. Gordon said that they inherited bearer bonds when they turned twenty-one. If Jackson is twenty-two now, he got his money within the year."

"If his father took him on that sea voyage to get him away from some sort of vice," Akara noted, "he wasted his time. That Tod seems so *sangfroid* probably influenced the old man into thinking that he'd help to straighten out Jacky-boy. I got a definite bad vibe from Tod. I had the funniest feeling that Norma was the mistress of the house and that Tod was the houseboy who serviced her. Maybe that's why he comes off as being so cool and confident. She's all the woman he needs, and Jackson is his compliant banker."

"Yes," George nodded. "I picked up on him, too. He's the puppet-master type. I don't think that twit Jackson is capable of scheming. If he did send the Portuguese translation of the will, he was probably scratching Tod's itch that he get Charles to settle the estate. We need to find out more about Jackson and his inheritance. How did he spend the money?" He sighed. "Charles and Gordon, both, need to watch their backs." He paused and then added, "And so do we."

MONDAY, JUNE 10, 2013

As Sensei was returning from delivering George and Akara to Philadelphia's International Airport his cellphone rang. He saw immediately that it was Father Willem deVries calling.

Sensei pulled over and parked.

"I wish I could give more and better news," deVries began, "but my contact in Lyon tells me that he has reached a dead end in Alaska. I made notes to be accurate. A Coast Guard cutter, the Choctaw, was shadowing an unidentified fishing vessel when it exploded. This was on 8 October 2012 off the coast of Attu in the Aleutian Islands. He says that the Naval Station on Attu was closed in 2010 and the population of 20 people - who were all associated with the station, left the island. It is completely deserted. The Choctaw spotted two dead men and a live woman lying inside some kind of floating wreckage. She was unconscious and badly injured. They picked her up and since there was a medic onboard she got emergency treatment. She was transferred to another Coast Guard ship, the Emory, that took her to the Alaskan mainland. Since she never regained consciousness while she was with either vessel, they had no way to identify her except to say that evidently the ship that exploded was a Chinese fishing vessel. They notified the Chinese authorities in Anchorage and took her to Providence Hospital there. She was admitted as a Jane Doe. And that was the end of the information line."

Sensei thanked him and slowly resumed his drive back to the temple. He entered the temple from the rear parking lot, and on his way past Akara's "sixteen server cluster" of computer "junk" - which it was to Sensei when Akara was not around to operate it - he cursed his own lack of technical skill, and knowing that it was still night time in Anchorage, he locked the temple and walked down to Wagner & Tilson's office. Beryl would know what he should do next.

Beryl Tilson made tea for Sensei in her apartment above their storefront office, and let him watch television while she dressed. She went down to the office and attended to her work until it was 9 a.m. in Anchorage. She then called Sensei to come downstairs, and as he nervously sat and listened, she called the hospital to get information about a Jane Doe admitted the previous October on or about the 9th or 10th. She learned that they divulged no information about any patient. If she had a serious or official request and could submit fingerprints of the subject patient when she presented her credentials and stated her request to the administrator, then maybe she could learn something. She was asked to understand that patient information was either privileged or impossible to give especially when having only sketchy data.

Beryl thanked the clerk. She turned to Sensei who had been listening to the conversation. "Do you have Sonya's fingerprints?"

Sensei could not think. "I don't know!"

"Did she ever give you her business card?"

"No."

"Did she ever send you a letter?"

"No. We communicated by phone, email, text."

"Did she ever look through your wallet?"

"No. Not that I ever saw."

"Am I correct in assuming that she has never been inside the temple or your apartment?"

"Yes. She's never been here at all."

Beryl called Martin Mazzavini, the attorney of a former client, in his Chicago office.

After going through three tiers of secretarial watchdogs, she got Martin on the line. "Marty, it is of extreme importance that we get fingerprints of Sonya Lee. Do you remember her?"

Martin Mazzavini said that he did indeed remember Sonya Lee.

"Do you have her business card or that letter she wrote your client that might have her fingerprints on it?"

"Let me get our technical guy in here." He instructed his secretary to summon someone to his office and to bring him the "Chang" files of the meeting which his grandfather attended. "That case is still being dragged-out with some of the compensation items," he told Beryl. "Can you wait on the line?"

"Yes. I'll wait... take your time. I've got nothing to do that's more important than this."

Martin lay the phone on his desk and Beryl and Sensei could hear him telling both his secretary and the technical assistant to put latex gloves on and to remove Sonya Lee's business card and that letter she had written in Arizona. "Dust them for prints. If you get two female prints, one from each, that match, prepare them for transmission." He picked up his phone. "Beryl, if we don't get lucky here, I can call the property manager where she lived in Tucson and send someone there to see if her prints are on her application."

"Good idea. We're drawing blanks up here. She had the use of a home in Malibu, but we don't have access to it. So yes... the Tucson place might still have her application." She took a deep breath. "So how's your family?"

"My grandfather asks for you regularly. He wants to know when you'll be in Chicago again."

"What? So he can be sure he's out of town?"

He laughed. "No, so he can brush up on his tango."

They talked casually for another few minutes. She heard a buzzing sound and Martin answer. "Wait," he said. Then he talked to Beryl. "We have a match between the two. He says they appear to be small... female. A complete right thumb on the card and a partial right thumb that has four points of match on the letter. Where do you want me to send the two specimens?"

"To my office computer. And Martin, thank you. You're an angel."

"I know. Come here and ruffle my feathers for me."

"*You have to ask me nicely*. Ciao." She could hear Martin laugh as she disconnected the call and touched Sensei's shoulder. "Let's turn on the big computer and see what we've got."

Sensei, armed with two fingerprints and all the photos he personally possessed of Sonya Lee booked a flight to Anchorage, Alaska.

This meant, of course, that Beryl had to watch both the office and the temple, full time.

TUESDAY, JUNE 11, 2013

Having spent all Monday flying to Johannesburg and staying overnight in a hotel in order to take a Tuesday morning flight to Maputo, the capital of Mozambique, George and Akara were trying to soak in as much of Africa as could be seen from the Maputo hotel window. Since their room faced east, what they could see of Africa was mostly the Madagascar Channel of the Indian Ocean.

The change from cosmopolitan South Africa to the only recently emerging democracy of Mozambique - that was younger than Akara Chatree - was startling. But the people seemed likable... nice, in fact. Akara's Portuguese, learned from his Brazilian mother, was barely recognizable in the colonial dialect; but at least, he assured George, he could read the signs.

Colonel Eusebio Machel, the man to whom they had to present their credentials, invited them into his office for a glass of iced tea. "We grow tea in Africa, you know," he said, "and coffee, too."

"Coffee's native to Africa, isn't it?" Akara asked, knowing that in fact it was.

"Yes. It takes a while to get the crop started, but even there we're making inroads. But you didn't come here to get a report from the Chamber of Commerce."

"No," George said. "We're here to investigate the murder of Devers Thompson." He regarded the middle-aged Colonel as a man who had mastered the art of seeming to know much more than he actually knew.

"Ah, yes. The American whose son was charged with his murder. After the defendant escaped, we had the father's body cremated. He was a very large man. Having the corpus delicti without the person accused of committing the act leaves things 'up in the air,' as we say. The accused and his companions left the country in the dead of night. There was no one to claim the body. Weeks later we received the results of the toxicology studies and learned that he had taken a large quantity of a sleeping drug before he was shot. All this would have been made public at trial. Frankly, I don't know what the law allows regarding the disposition of the remains. If someone wants to claim them, and if the law permits us to release them, well, let me look into it. See me again before you leave Mozambique. Perhaps I'll have an answer then. With proper authorization and payment of some kind of fee, it may be possible for you to take his ashes back to the United States."

"We'll check with our client and ask him if he'd like to fax you an authorization. Possibly, he will want to talk to you, himself."

"Who is your client? Gordon Thompson?"

"No. Charles Thompson, the executor of the estate of his brother, Devers. I feel certain that he'll want us to bring back the ashes. I understand that you'll have to do a good deal of consultation with various government entities. These things are never simple."

"By all means have Mr. Thompson call me. If he agrees, then perhaps we can have the container prepared and all the paperwork completed before you leave Mozambique. Until now, we had no one to contact regarding the disposition of the remains. We knew only of the accused, Gordon, and his brother Jackson who was hardly qualified to act as a consultant in such a matter. They shared the same home address." He picked up a pencil and began to drum on his desk blotter. "But tell me... if you're investigating Devers' death, you must have other suspects in mind. Do you?"

"A hunch," George said. "I don't need to tell a law enforcement officer that hunches are usually worthless."

"What about the other brother? It wasn't my case, but from what little I've heard he seems to be more the type."

"That would be my hunch."

"Mine, too, Mr. Wagner. Originally, mine, too. But then I had one of my men in Manica Province verify Jackson's presence there at the time of the murder. He evidently did spend the day in the bush and got lucky by encountering a young, ferocious nomadic male - a rogue - which he shot. He proceeded to celebrate the kill to the point of public intoxication the likes of which few residents had ever seen. He was suspiciously energetic."

"Might that energy be ascribed to drugs?" George asked.

"It certainly might have been, but no one we talked to had any ideas about where he obtained the drugs. The assumption was that if he had any drugs, he had brought them with him."

"What made you renew your intention to try Gordon?" Akara asked.

"We had two reasons. The day after Gordon escaped from jail, I got the report on the gas tank contents of the rented fishing boat. The owner refilled the tank and the amount of fuel he had to put in equalled exactly the mile out and mile back trip that Gordon claimed. That ship did not go out a second time.

"We also received a certified Portuguese translation of the father's will which named both boys as his heirs. But, as I've said, I had already ruled Jackson out as a suspect and also as anyone with whom we could reasonably communicate.

"It's a well-known story around here. Jackson's conduct on the hunt was reprehensible. Evidently, when confronted with an old toothless lion who hangs around one of the camps and eats what's left on the plates of the guests, Jackson got so scared that his bowels actually moved. That such a man would shoot a man in the water... like a fish in a barrel... would seem in character, except that our investigation ruled him out. But I did assume that it was Jackson who mailed me the translated copy of the will. I wrote back to the 'Interested in Justice' party, General Delivery, who sent it, saying that he'd have to verify its authenticity here. And then, I think, we would have had him here to answer questions. Perhaps he would have implicated Gordon further."

"I doubt that Jackson would ever place himself in jeopardy. I think he would send his attorney to testify about the will."

"Probably. But then we'd have to think of some other ruse. Where are you off to, now?" Machel asked.

"To Beira, " George answered.

Machel stood up. "Keep me posted."

Akara extended his hand. "*Obrigado. Você foi muito gentil e prestativa.*"

Eusebio Machel looked pleasantly surprised. "*Estamos aqui para servir. Por favor, deixe-me saber se eu posso ajudá-lo novamente.*" Then he looked at George and asked, "*Onde você está indo agora?*"

Akara answered. "Our destination is Manica Province, Coutada 9. *Nós gostaríamos de falar com a agência que contratou com Jackson.*

"*Você sabe o nome da agência de Safari?*" asked Machel.

"Yes," Akara replied. "We believe he booked his safari with O'Della's agency."

Machel stood up and shook hands with George and Akara. He gave them each one of his official business cards. "*Boa sorte.* When you meet the agents at O'Della's, tell them Eusebio Machel sends his regards."

"Tell me," George turned and asked, "has Jackson's missing Browning rifle ever turned up?"

"Not to my knowledge. The Browning .375 is a fine rifle. I hope it's not lying in the mud someplace."

As they left the office, George asked, "Just what did you commit us to?"

"Nothing. I told him we were going to Manica Province to interview the safari company who handled Jackson's trip. He wished us good luck."

"We'll probably need it. The question is, should we check out of our hotel room here or keep it even after we take our flight to Beira?"

"If we're voting on it, I say let's keep it. I feel more comfortable knowing I've got a place to retreat to."

Sensei had never been to Alaska before. He had a window seat and the entire time he flew over the seam between the Canadian and U.S. wilderness that was punctuated with little towns and highway scars, he felt as though he were heading for a foreign country. The feeling intensified as he flew over the Rockies, Coast Mountains, and glaciers; and when he finally landed in Anchorage, he instinctively patted his shirt's breast pocket to be sure his passport was there.

Carrying his overnight bag, he walked down the jetway and was slightly surprised that nothing else impeded him from leaving the terminal and getting into a cab. "I've got a reservation at the LaFitte Arms Hotel. I'll just run in there and drop off my bag and come right out, and then you can take me to Providence Hospital," he said. The driver simply put up the fare flag and began to drive.

"You understand," said the hospital administrator whose desk plaque indicated that her name was Tess Blancaneau, "that we have privacy rules. We can't just give out information about our patients."

Sensei put several photographs of Sonya and himself together and the two fingerprint exemplars on her desk. "Her name is Sonya Lee, she was an agent, now retired, with Hong Kong Customs. A U.S. Coastguard cutter named the Choctaw, picked her up when a ship they were tailing exploded at sea on October 8, 2012. They transferred her to another vessel, The Emory, that brought her finally to your hospital. She's a Chinese national and she was unconscious when she was admitted as a Jane Doe."

"What is your relationship to her?"

"She is the only woman I have ever loved. That is, as far as I'm concerned, closer than a blood relationship. Please help me to find her."

Ms. Blancaneau looked at the photographs and, convinced that Sensei was being truthful, asked him to give his passport to her and to sit in the waiting room while she contacted "the right people."

After an hour, she appeared in the waiting room's doorway. Returning his passport, photos and the fingerprint card, she said, "I can tell you that on December 6th, Miss Lee regained consciousness. A representative of the Chinese consulate had already been here in October and had taken her right hand fingerprints - Miss Lee's left arm had been amputated while she was on board the Choctaw. It had been crushed, apparently, during the explosion. The medical report from the Choctaw said merely that certain veins and arteries had been tied off and the skin closed and she was given blood... O positive. She was also burned."

Sensei had stood up when Ms. Blancaneau entered the room. As she spoke his stomach began to churn and a copious amount of saliva filled his mouth. His head began to feel warm and his thoughts could not focus. First he sat down and then just as she said, "burned," he got up and bolted to the men's room door that was at the end of the waiting room. Ms. Blancaneau sent a hospital orderly into the men's room to assist him. Fifteen minutes later they emerged, the orderly holding Sensei's left arm around his own neck and his right arm circling Sensei's waist. "I'll be all right," Sensei assured him. "It was just the shock." The orderly dumped him into a chair. "What else can you tell me about her?" Sensei asked Ms. Blancaneau.

"She regained consciousness in December. Her foot injury - she also lost her left foot" - the orderly who had been walking out of the room stopped and turned around to see if he'd be needed for *that* news - "had healed. But without consciousness there was no physical therapy available for her. At any rate, her facial burns had healed and there was nothing more we could do for her. Two men from the Chinese consulate signed her out on December 22nd and paid her hospital bill which, I can tell you, was considerable. Where they took her, I do not know." She wrote the consulate's address on a piece of paper.

Sensei took the paper and put it in his pocket without looking at it. "Was she rational when she left?"

"Rational? I didn't speak to her myself but evidently she was sufficiently aware of her surroundings to ask for the Chinese officials to come and get her."

Sensei thanked her and, staggering slightly, walked out of the hospital and got into a waiting cab.

The Chinese consulate was not open for business. Sensei learned this when he walked up to the entryway and was confronted by a uniformed

Chinese soldier. The sign indicated that the consul's hours were 9 a.m. to 3 p.m. It was ten minutes after five. As he returned to his hotel he could see that the afternoon sun was still shining brightly.

While George and Akara stood on the station platform waiting for the train that went inland to Chimoio, Manica Province's capital city, to pull into the station, George called Charles Thompson and discussed the acquisition of Devers' remains. He gave Machel's phone and fax numbers to Charles and suggested that he call him directly to conduct the negotiations.

Charles agreed and was, in fact, talking to Eusebio Machel even as George and Akara were finally boarding the train.

Akara, sitting at the window seat, was delighted to see so many Portuguese signs, but was disappointed to find so little else of Brazilian culture in evidence, except for a few food dishes sold at the station stops. The scenery, a spectacular mix of jungle, marsh, savannah, high plains, and granite hills, surprised them, just as the "quick" food served on the train was of first class quality. Akara bought bags of "sweet and salty" Brazilian cashew nuts. "My weakness," he explained.

At Chimoio, they checked in with the local police department. At first, George let Akara do all of the talking. Asked by Police Captain Raul Mtindi if he were armed, George showed a two-inch penknife that hung on his keychain. The police chief laughed and told Akara that since the knife was suitable only for hunting mice he didn't have to register it. "And mice," he said in English, "are not endangered. You may kill all you want."

George ignored the levity. He took photographs of the lion's head and of Jackson posing with the dead beast and laid them on the Chief's desk. "Do you know this animal?" he asked.

"Only the one with the rifle."

The remark surprised George. "I take it that you didn't approve of Jackson Thompson."

"He was drugged and he was drunk. He lost his rifle and charged every man he encountered with being the thief who stole it. He crossed the frontier to go on a canned hunt in Zimbabwe and bribed a handful of poor fellows to bring the beast's carcass back into my country. But, of course, he denied that he had gone into Zimbabwe and 'let it slip' that he had gone on the hunt here in my jurisdiction. I'm sorry that it took his father's death to get him out of here, but that's life." He handed the photographs to George. "Now if you'll excuse me I have work to do."

"One question, Captain. Has Jackson's rifle ever turned up?"

"If it has ever been found, it would be unlikely that after all the trouble he caused, it would be turned into this office." He got up from his desk and began to walk into a rear office.

As he pushed open the door, George caught the captain furtively gesturing to one of the officers who was sitting quietly at a desk. By the time he and Akara were out onto the sidewalk, he could see the man get up and begin to follow them. "Don't look around," George said, "but we're being followed. Let's just keep on going to Maudsley's Taxidermy Shop. They've got to know that that's where we're headed. So why the hell are they following us?"

"Maybe," Akara ventured, "they're going to see if we find a third explanation for the lion's death. Machel says it was the 'lucky shot' of a wild rogue in the Mozambique bush. Mtindi says he shot it in a Zimbabwe canned hunt. What is a third possibility? Something tells me that they don't want it to be a canned hunt in Mozambique."

Taxidermist Gregory Maudsley cautiously stood in his display room and examined George's credentials and looked through his photographs. He pointed with admiration at the lion's head that hung in the den of the Thompson house. "I severed the beast's head," he said proudly. "The mane is exceptionally dark. The darker the mane, the more dominant the male... more testosterone in his system. He was a young rogue. And that is a beautiful mounting, if I must say so." He indicated that they should enter a small alcove in his shop.

"The art of taxidermy is dying," Maudsley said. "This freeze-dry business is finishing us off. Even where the ruminants are hunted and the meat is given to the poor, they arrange to ship the head to a freeze-dry company. It's expensive, but frankly, it does look better, although, I'm told, it tends to get buggy." He looked at Akara's photographs of the trophy. "Beautiful work," he said, enviously. "But I don't want to talk about the incident." He returned the photographs. "I'm sorry. Enough damage has already been done around here because of that lion."

"Why don't you open your own freeze-dry company?" Akara asked.

"Capital. Who has the capital?"

"Tell us what we need to know and I'll see to it that you're given the capital... and even a few men from Italy who know how to perform the work."

"You'll pay for it?" He chuckled incredulously.

"I could... or I could let Gordon Thompson whose life you'd be saving, have the honor of paying for it." He took out his iPhone and showed Maudsley photographs of himself and Gordon Thompson both formally dressed and posed elegantly with Norma Beckridge. "Either way, tell us what we need to know and the freeze-dry company will be Maudsley's Ltd. of Chimoio."

"Gordon? Isn't he the one who was blamed?" Maudsley asked.

"Yes. And he's innocent."

"And who do you think killed the father?"

"It's a little too soon to point a finger at the guilty party," Akara conceded, "but the person who would benefit most is the man who killed that lion."

Maudsley laughed. "That man, I assure you, is innocent."

"Oh? I take it you mean that Jackson Thompson did not shoot the beast. We're here to learn exactly what Jackson did do. So, please, tell us what happened. We'll keep your confidence," Akara said, "and you'll still get the freeze-dry business."

George leaned back against a display case and, pleasantly amused, let Akara conduct the interview. The kid, he told himself, was doing fine.

Maudsley unfolded chairs and placed them in front of his visitors. As everyone sat down, he explained, "Ah, that Jackson fella got the poop scared out of him when a toothless old lion came looking for scraps at the breakfast table. He dropped ammo all over the ground as he climbed up on the table and tried to load his rifle. Everybody was laughing about it. The cat's nails are worn down from walking on concrete. His teeth are gone. A child can climb on his back and he'll tolerate him for ten meters. But he's too weak to take him farther. This poor creature terrified Jackson.

"One of the guides knew that he had paid the safari agency a considerable sum to kill a lion and that the man was unfit to go on safari. He correctly surmised that Jackson wouldn't want to return to civilization empty-handed, so he offered him a way out... a shameful way out.

"A few hours later, Jackson comes in here with a man pushing a cart filled with the big male. 'I only want the head,' he says.

"This is not the way an animal killed in the bush is transported. I see that the animal has been struck twice. One was a grazing shot over the left flank and the other was the slug of a .450 Bushmaster in his lung. I had already heard about the breakfast incident and happened to know that the ammo Jackson spilled was .375 Winchester. I definitely didn't want to work on an animal from a canned hunt. It's not smart to get mixed up with people like that. I expressed my reluctance to take the job, but Jackson says, 'Do you want to get paid to cut off the head or not?' He wasn't the one who pushed the cart, and that fellow... a big guy with a bad reputation, is still standing there waiting for me to answer. I didn't think he wanted to push the cart to another taxidermist, so I say, 'All right. Dead is dead.' And I agree to sever the head. 'What do you want with the carcass?' I ask. And Jackson says, 'Destroy it.'"

George grinned. "So that was the great white hunter we met last week... the one in these pictures."

Maudsley looked again at the couple of photos that Jackson was in. "Yes, that's the man. But that's not all."

"Oh?" Akara asked. "*Conte-nos a história real.*"

Maudsley whispered, "*Vou dar-lhe a prova, mas não dou o meu nome.*"

"Your name will come up only in terms of the freeze-dry business."

"I had the cart-man put the animal in the big refrigerator. I told Jackson to come back the following day to pick up the head. I don't like to keep the wormy guts in there so as soon as they left I gutted the animal. And then something told me to look into its stomach contents. So I did. And I found sausages and a couple of vertebrae that had been sawed through with a band saw."

"Oh!" George exclaimed. "So you definitely could prove that it was a captive lion he killed. A 'canned hunt.' Jesus!"

"From Mozambique's own animal reserves?" Akara asked.

"No! There is a new industry in our rich neighbor to the South. Along with South Africa's luxury hotels, tourism, and international interests, they've gone into the lion breeding business. They have dozens of petting zoos where tourists can come to feed a lion cub with a baby bottle. The cub's mother has teats and could feed her own cubs, but the tourists wouldn't pay money to watch that from a safe distance. The tourists are told the cubs have been abandoned or rescued, but in truth, the cubs have been removed from their mother so that she can go into heat again quickly and make more cubs.

"People love getting their photos taken while bottle-feeding a cub or romping in the grass with a couple of playful little lions. But the cubs grow up fast and so they supply 'canned hunt' operators with young male lions for cowards to come and, in a safely fenced area, shoot a lion that's just been released from a cage... a young lion who has always regarded human beings as his friends. They have so many house-bred male lions for their cheap 'safaris' that the supply exceeds the demands. And they sell the surplus to canned operators in nearby countries and bribe a few poor border guards. Do you see the damage this does?"

"No," Akara said. "Not really. A hunter pays a canned hunt operator to shoot a canned lion. It seems like a closed system."

"Let me tell you the price that's paid. And it is not a closed system. Mozambique authorities know that it's vital to keep predator and prey in perfect balance. Lions on one side and the ruminants - antelope, wildebeest, zebra, giraffe on the other. They calculate the number of licenses they'll issue for trophy animals.

"Now, there are always two or three adult males in a pride. Which males are hunted? Not those... but the rogue males that have been driven away from the pride: a young adult or an old alpha male who was defeated by a stronger male. Male lions are not good hunters. The lioness, yes, she's a great team hunter. The best! But rogue males, especially, pick on the most vulnerable prey: human beings, goats and cubs. The animal rights people don't want to tell you how many people in Tanzania, our neighbor to the North, are attacked by rogue male lions from the Serengeti. Not a week passes but someone is mauled. So issuing licenses for trophy male lions is beneficial. It keeps the populations in balance. Before a wild lion begins killing the helpless, a real hunter brings him down in the wild.

"When Mozambique issues a man a license and he uses that license to kill an imported cat, the local rogue lion population grows by one. And if there are ten canned hunts, multiply that one by ten. And the rogue keeps killing until he's brought down. There are records of a single rogue killing as many as thirty-five people. Domestic animals are easy prey, too. The rogues will also surveil the pride and when the father goes out to mark the boundaries of his territory and the mothers go out to hunt, the rogue males come in and kill the cubs. This is not sport anymore."

"I see," Akara said. "I hadn't thought of it that way. So, where do they keep these imported cats? Jackson could not have gone that far to kill his."

George interjected, "It's got to be a secretive affair. No trophy hunter will go home and brag that he shot a captive lion."

"That's right," said Maudsley. "So the people who operate these enclosures may poach antelope and gazelles to feed a caged lion, or, since they have to operate close to civilization - there's little sense in being in the distant bush - more than likely they feed the caged animals old unsalable *churrasco* sausage or whatever they can get from the garbage of restaurants. There are big game parks in our southern neighbor. Such canned hunts are legal there. But here, if such an operation is conducted, the place must be hidden and, by definition, that means small. And then they turn an animal loose in what is somebody's back yard and the hunter shoots him. It's a wonder that they don't allow the 'hunter' to shoot him while he's still in the cage! In a few cases I've heard of, when the hunter is still scared or is a bad shot, they'll help him out and kill the cat for him. This is shameful to the point of criminality."

"And Jackson Thompson needed to be helped by the other rifle?" Akara laughed. "What a fraud he is."

"Yes," Maudsley sighed, "the sad thing is that these petting-zoo cats don't *become* rogues... they're *born* rogues. They're never going to belong to a pride. These breeders are like so many Fagins... raising the innocent to be sacrificed to their greed. Somebody opens the cage door, the cat goes outside alone for the first time since he was young, and some coward shoots him."

Akara laughed and quoted Dickens. "'A friend's just an enemy in disguise.'"

"Who said that," George asked. "Bill Sikes?"

"No, the Artful Dodger."

"What happens to the females that get old? The excess females?" George asked.

"They recycle the meat. When cubs cease to bottle feed they eat meat and grow big enough for tourists to romp in the grass with them. And I guess that since she hasn't lived in the wild, her hide is free of scars and such and would make a nice rug... something to put before the fireplace."

"Where does the fear of getting mixed up with these canned hunt operators come in?" George asked.

"They're making big money and don't want anyone to disturb their profits. Foreign governments have raped this country, Mr. Wagner. Only in recent years are we becoming self-sufficient. One thing we have maintained is the integrity of our safari industry. A lion taken in Mozambique is a lion truly hunted, man against a fearsome, destructive beast. Slick operators and cowards like Jackson Thompson can only destroy our reputation. Canned hunts must not be allowed to operate here!"

"I can readily appreciate that, Mr. Maudsley. But as to our specific mission, we're interested in Jackson's time element," George said. "On what day did this happen with the cart?"

"On the same day that he arrived here. After witnessing Jackson dancing on the table, the guide knew he could never go into the bush, and he happened to know of one of these illegal lion habitats. They took a ride in a truck, shot the beast, drove it to the cart-man a few blocks from here, and brought it to my shop.

"After I gutted the animal and saw the sausage and butchered bones, I sacked the guts and put them in the freezer and went home. It was the next morning that I went in to work on the animal in the cooler. I skinned the cat and froze the hide, too. I decapitated him crudely and then brought the head out and finessed the cuts so that he could send it to be freeze-dried. I packaged the head in ice. I gave the meat to some native people. They know how to cook it. I can't tell you what it tastes like. I've never been hungry enough."

"And you still have the evidence? The hide and the guts?" George inquired.

"Yes. I wanted to make a case for reinforcing the ban against these illegal hunts, but then I found out that my brother-in-law works for one of them. I kept everything in case I was needed at the trial."

"What?" George laughed. "Against your brother-in-law?"

"That would have been the greater evil." He laughed. "Actually, I kept them because I figured that they might have something to do with the Thompson murder that was on the news that day, and I might be needed to testify at the trial. Jackson had paid me by American Express. I knew his name. But then his brother Gordon escaped, and I just held onto them."

George turned to Akara. "As long as he had them this long, let's let him keep them till all this is settled. But first let's see them for ourselves."

"As you wish," Maudsley said, leading them back to his walk-in refrigerator. "They're in a bag in the freezer compartment."

They couldn't unroll the animal's frozen hide, but they could see a plastic bag that contained the .450 slug. Ice had crystalized around the stomach, but Maudsley wiped it away to reveal a four-inch piece of *churrasco* sausage. Akara photographed the hide and the stomach contents and also the yellow tag that bore the name, "Thompson, Jackson. 3 setembro. 2012."

George paid the taxidermist to keep the "chain of custody" intact and said he'd be contacting him in the near future. "One thing more," George asked, "just to be specific. What time of day did Jackson bring the lion here?"

"It was before lunch. My guess would be about eleven o'clock."

"Then at dawn he left the ship and was in Chimoio for breakfast. After breakfast he was taken to the canned hunt where he shot the beast and was brought back to Chimoio to the big fellow's house who put it in a cart and wheeled it here by eleven o'clock. Would he have had time to return to Beira that day in your opinion?"

"Money buys silence. He could have hired a driver to take him down to Beira. If the driver waited for him, he could have been back the same day. If he flew, it's half an hour one way."

Outside, Akara ventured, "And so, after Jackson dropped the cat off here, he could have returned to Beira, killed his father, and then returned to Chimoio to claim the head and go back again to the ship."

"That's only what it looks like. Let's check into a hotel and have a few beers," George said. "We have to talk to the O'Della Safari people, and we still have to get back to Beira to talk to those two men, particularly the one who claimed he saw Devers Thompson return in the cabin cruiser with Gordon."

They checked into a hotel and were directed to the rooftop bar and grill. As they climbed up onto the roof they could look in the distance and see the savannah's tall ocher grass wave in the wind as if some divine hand were stroking it. A single tree stood alone like a tiny island. "Why," Akara asked, "do you always see just one isolated tree in the landscape?"

"I don't know," George answered. "I've often wondered about that, myself."

After leaving the consulate, Sensei returned to his hotel and stopped in the hotel restaurant. He ordered soup and bread for dinner. He ate a little of the soup and then realized that he was not hungry. Knowing that for his stomach's sake, he should eat the bread, he folded it into a paper napkin and put it in his pocket.

He called Beryl but his call went to voicemail and he correctly assumed that in both his and George's absence, she was being over-burdened with work and might even be sleeping.

"I've got to think," he told himself, returning to his room. He lay on his bed, unable to think at all of anything except how Sonya must have suffered... how if she were still alive she would still be suffering. "You'll never be able to put your feet in those Manolo Blahnik red spiked heels," he said aloud. "Ah, one shoe would be enough. Sonny. Sonny..."

When, according to his own Philadelphia time, it was past midnight, he fell asleep, emotionally exhausted.

WEDNESDAY, JUNE 12, 2013

At 8 a.m. Beryl returned Sensei's call. He told her that the consulate had been closed and that he would be returning to it shortly.

"Frankly," Beryl said, "it's good you didn't see them. They're at the top of the food chain, and if they turn you down, nobody else will give you a bite. The Chinese consul paid her bills and signed her out. You've got problems in two ways: her injuries may make her want to keep hidden; and her security clearances and the data stored in her brain may make the Chinese want to keep her hidden."

"I don't know what to do next."

"The best way to get information is to call in a marker. The Philippine Ambassador to Panama knows you and, indirectly, Sonya from the case we worked on last year. He isn't going to lie for you, but he does owe you a favor and he does have a legitimate reason for asking Sonya a question or two. Call him in Panama City, tell him your problem, and ask if he'll help you by contacting the Chinese embassy in Washington to ask where a representative of his government could contact her. That's the best I can come up with. Check the time difference before you call Panama."

Sensei searched his phone log and got the number of the Philippine Ambassador in Panama. He had to explain who he was and what the nature of his call was to several clerks and assistants before the Ambassador answered the phone. Fortunately, he remembered well the case that Sensei had worked on. He listened to Sensei's story and agreed to help. "I will give you this advice: stay in your hotel room. I'll contact the Chinese Ambassador's office and explain to one of his aides that Sonya Lee was last known to be in a hospital in Anchorage, Alaska last December. I'll ask if he can tell me where she can be found now. I'll explain that she was instrumental in solving the illegal organ donation racket in the Philippines last year, a case that involved a Chinese national. He'll know what I'm referring to. The routine usually is that with approval, the Ambassador's clerk will contact the consular chief in Anchorage and if they're willing to provide details, they'll tell him and he'll tell me and then I'll have my secretary call you. Be prepared to be patient. Buy yourself some novels to catch up on your reading while you wait."

Sensei went to a bookstore and bought half a dozen novels none of which he expected to be able to think clearly enough to read, and walked back to his hotel room.

"Now I wait," he said aloud, and turned on the TV.

George and Akara's first stop was O'Della's Safari Company, the agents who provided the hunting services to Jackson Thompson in Manica Province.

O'Della's offices were within walking distance of the hotel and George was happy to walk the few blocks just to get his leg stretched. They were not dressed in the garments of outdoorsmen. It was windy and their shoes were covered in dust before they got to the office.

"Are you here to book a safari?" the receptionist asked as she looked admiringly at Akara.

"Now who," Akara asked, "would want to go out there in the bush to look at anything when he could stand right here and look at a pretty girl like you?" George nudged him.

The receptionist giggled. "I don't think you answered my question."

George answered. "We're private investigators. Colonel Eusebio Machel knows we're here and sends his regards. We have only a few questions regarding a hunt for lion that an American named Jackson Thompson took with your company last September."

The girl excused herself and walked into the rear offices. When she returned, a tall English gentleman followed her. "I booked Thompson's hunt," he said. "I'm Lionel Darrow, office manager. Come back to my office and perhaps I can help you. Did he register any complaints?"

"No," said George, handing Darrow his business card. "I just saw him a week ago and he was telling everyone how exciting the trip was. We have questions about his experiences and the amount of time he was actually in the bush looking for lion. He does not have a reputation for bravery."

"Mr. Wagner," Darrow said portentously, "I have met men who were foolishly brave. Until I met Jackson Thompson, I had never met a man who was foolishly cowardly." He began to laugh. "He was all dressed up and well-armed for the bush. I'm sure he looks great in photographs. But the reality..." He sighed. "Are you here about the murder?"

"Yes. We're investigating the death of Devers Thompson."

"The prevailing opinion around here is that the wrong son was charged. The murder of a tourist is never good for business. The only break we had was that it was his son... and not a citizen... who was charged with the crime. We let 'sleeping dogs' lie and didn't attempt to interfere."

"Well," George consoled him, "Jackson is playing-up the great safari experience he had here, so any bad P.R. about the murder has probably been off-set." He placed a copy of the photo of Jackson posing with the dead lion on Darrow's desk.

"Ah." Darrow seemed genuinely surprised. "And this is the cat he got?" He paused to examine the photographs closely. "I'm glad Jackson is such a good liar. If he told the truth about his experiences here, it also would not be good for business."

"What happened?" Akara asked.

Darrow leaned back in his chair and put his hands behind his head. "This is a fun trip down Memory Lane. Locally, it's one of our favorite stories. On the third day of September - we all remember the day - he showed up with a kit that anyone would envy. A fine Browning rifle... hunter's garments Hemingway would have wanted. As it happens, there is an old toothless lion–"

"Machel told us!" George and Akara joined Darrow in laughing about the incident.

Darrow continued. "People have suggested that we euthanize the poor beast. But he's become as tame as an old pussy cat that likes his neck scratched. We feed him soft foods. He can't chew. We put the uneaten foods in a bowl and he literally licks his dinner. Next step will be a baby bottle."

They laughed again, knowing what was coming next in the story.

"Anyway, there was Jackson, dressed like the great Bwana of Tarzan films, and Buddy - that's the lion's name - happened to come towards the picnic area where breakfast was being served, and Jackson tried to load the Browning as he climbed up onto the table. The cook was furious. The food had just been brought out and had to be thrown away because Jackson stepped on the serving dishes. One of the guides grabbed the rifle and pushed Jackson off the table. He shouted at Jackson, 'You have hurt Buddy's feelings, but thanks to your dirty boots, you've given him a good breakfast.' All the food was placed in Buddy's bowls. Jackson had soiled his pants and had to change his clothes. The safari was not off to a good start. More food was brought, but a few Dutchmen declined to sit at the same table with him. It was disgraceful. The professional hunter who was to accompany him into the bush refused to accept the responsibility for him and, unfortunately, no other P.H. cared to associate himself with Jackson."

"Did you know that he brought the lion's head home?"

"I heard that he shipped it out to be freeze dried."

"Did you hear the rumor that the lion was the victim of a canned hunt?" George grinned.

"Ahhh... touchy subject." He chuckled. "Let's just say there was a rumor that he bought a freshly killed lion from a hunter who had broken his leg and needed the money for his hospital bills."

"That rumor - at least the part of freeze drying the head - is true. I myself saw the lion's head. Here," George opened to the photographs and slid his iPhone across Darrow's desk, "is a picture of me standing next to it. Look at them all. They were taken a week ago."

"Could I copy these photos?" Darrow asked.

"Certainly."

Akara opened his iPhone. "Here's more. I can transfer them all to your computer if you like." Darrow indicated that he'd like that very much and got up to let Akara sit in his chair, and in a few minutes all the transfers were completed.

"Do you know who did the freeze drying?" Darrow asked.

"Giacalone in Milan. I checked them out. They're a very reputable company."

"Yes, and they do the extras. If a lion is missing a tooth, they insert a plastic one that looks so much like a real tooth that you can't tell which is which. I think they must use one of their famous hair stylists to get the mane looking like that. Seriously, they shampoo and blow dry the mane. I guess they put creme rinse on it." He began to laugh.

"Do old lions go bald?" George asked, laughing.

"They usually don't live that long to find out," Browning chuckled. "Buddy's hair is rather ratty looking, though he's far from bald. But if one did need hair, I'm sure Giacalone's would give him a few hair plugs."

"The damned thing sure is impressive hanging on a wall." It was obvious that Darrow did not want to discuss canned hunts. "Did you know that Gordon joked that he and his father were fishing for coelacanth?" George asked.

With that, all three men laughed again, and George and Akara stood up. Darrow asked, "What's your next stop?"

"We'll probably have a look around. Maybe take one of those tourist rides out into the bush."

"You might want to invest in some less business-like clothing," Darrow suggested.

"We've brought jeans and cowboy boots with us," Akara said. "Without rifles we don't need places for extra magazines or bandolier belts."

"Change and meet me back at Grady's Bar. I'll stake you to a couple of cold beers. They keep some cold for Americans. We'll map out a tour of the savannah and scrub jungle. I've got a Land Rover and can show you places that the tourists don't usually see."

They returned to their hotel, changed their clothes, and went to spend a couple of hours with Lionel Darrow. They learned only that Jackson's cowardice had become the stuff of legends. No one wanted to talk about the source of the beautifully maned lion in the photos which Darrow showed everyone. They did accept the invitation to go into the bush early the following morning and see sights, Darrow insisted, that no man should ever miss.

On their way back to the hotel they passed a pawn shop that had rifles for sale. "Let's see if Jackson's rifle made the pawn scene," George said.

Then went into the shop and exhausted the manager's patience by looking at the stocks of all the Brownings. None had the initials JT carved into it.

THURSDAY, JUNE 13, 2013

The morning was brilliant in Chimoio and from the rooftop cafe of their hotel they could see a dozen different landscapes - from the green carpet of lowland jungle, to the high tawny ocean of grass undulating with the western breeze, and the granite outcrops that announced the distant hills. "This is one beautiful place," Akara said.

Both Akara and George were dressed in cowboy boots and jeans and carried binoculars. Although the morning was cool, they did not bring jackets as they went down to meet Lionel Darrow for a ride through the savannah.

"A few hundred miles north of us," Darrow informed them as they drove, "the Serengeti offers every kind of animal... from Nile crocs to hippos and rhinos. But here, it's mostly ungulates and the big male cats. Hunting lion is far more dangerous than people think. We do have luxury camps where the hunter's family can get first class accommodations; but during the hunt, the hunter sleeps in a tent in the bush.

"Yes, it's dangerous. Throughout the savannah there are large areas of riparian jungle in which the big cats can hide; and during the day the cats sleep. They're not nocturnal, they're crepuscular - twilight hunters with great night vision eyes. And it's the female who does the hunting. The alpha male does allow a couple of adolescent or subservient males to stay in the pride, but his job is to mark his territory and to roar away other predatory animals. When he's replaced in combat - usually after three years - he becomes a wounded rogue and then the winner often kills the loser's cubs. The younger males that are driven out of the pride and these former-alpha males are the ones that are hunted on safaris. Incidentally, lions don't suffocate their prey, as most people think. They bite down on the neck and shut off the blood supply to the brain. It's a chokehold done with canines. This is much faster than suffocation. But they will suffocate the prey as a last resort."

He drove up a rocky outcrop to a parking area on top which gave a spectacular view of the landscape and the distant Buzi River and jungle. Herds of water buffalo, zebras, and antelope grazed in seeming contentment while, off to the side under a solitary tree a pride of lions snoozed in the shade. "Makes you wonder," Darrow said quietly, "why God gave man dominion over the animals. They seem to be so peaceful."

"At least until twilight," George said quietly.

Suddenly, from a large granite monolith a hundred meters away, a shot was fired. The radiator of the Land Rover was struck and the water squirted out as Akara, George, and Lionel Darrow dove for cover behind the car.

"Who the hell is shooting at us?" George snapped at Darrow as if he expected that Darrow would know.

"I have no clue. None. Nobody's ever shot at me before."

Akara tried to be philosophical. "We haven't been here long enough to make any enemies."

Darrow, peeking from the side of the Land Rover quickly responded, "How much time do you need?"

"Easy," George said, taking out his cellphone and seeing immediately that he could not get a signal. "Maybe they think we're somebody else. But whether or not they've got the right target, we're out here in the middle of nowhere with a car we can't drive and no cellphone service. How much trouble are we in if they just left us here?"

"I've got a rifle and a satellite phone in the car. I can call for help and if anyone advances on us, I'm a good shot. So keep your eyes open." He looked at his binoculars with disgust. "These were recently submerged in water and haven't been the same. Lend me yours a minute."

Akara gave him his binoculars. Darrow studied the monolith. "George, take a look at the lower right of the rock. Does that look like the ass end of a vehicle?"

George studied the rock. "Yes. It looks like the truck bed of a red pickup truck, to be exact."

"I thought so. That's one of the bastards who were operating a canned zoo." He crawled into the Land Rover and reached into the glove compartment for his satellite phone. When he tried to turn it on, he discovered that the battery had been removed and the entire battery connection had been torn out. "The phone's been destroyed." He flopped on the ground beside Akara and showed him the ruined interior of the phone. "This was a well-planned ambush. We're in deep shit."

"How are we fixed for water?" George asked.

"I keep a few gallons in the Rover," Darrow replied as he reached inside and grabbed one of the bottles. "Let's hope they didn't dump salt inside." He removed the cap and took a swig. "It seems ok to me. You try it."

George took a large swallow of water and handed the jug to Akara. "It tastes ok... but I can name half a dozen poisons that are odorless and tasteless."

"Unless we see that truck move, we're stuck here... pinned down. They could keep us here until sundown and then let the lions have their fun with us. The hyenas will come first and give our position away. We'll be safe inside the car.

"When will your people start to miss you and come looking for you?" George asked.

"By tomorrow morning. Although without my GPS on, they may take awhile to find us."

Akara looked at them quizzically. "Excuse me, Gentlemen, but I don't particularly feel like being a sitting duck out here. You've got a rifle. Can't you shoot the rear tires of that truck? Why should they be free to leave us here? If they have to call for help, we've got a better chance of being located."

George and Lionel Darrow looked at each other. "Why not?" Darrow said. "I just zeroed-in my scope this morning. How many shots do you think I'll need? What's the bet?"

"Two," George said. "With a little luck you'll hit the gas tank."

"If I can't do that, I'll buy dinner. If I can, you buy."

Darrow lay belly down on the ground, put a rock under the barrel, adjusting it until he sighted the rear of the truck. He fired two shots and the truck exploded. Immediately two men began to run out from behind the huge rock. Akara watched them in his binoculars. "One is hobbling. He's hurt. The other has a rifle," he said.

"Let's just keep watching," Darrow said, "and see what they do." Huge clouds of black smoke rose into the sky. "Between the noise and the smoke, we ought to attract any human beings who are within a ten mile radius."

"Quite possibly," George noted, "their GPS indicator was inside the truck that just blew up. They're in the same predicament as we. Maybe worse. We're unhurt and we have water."

"The one that's hurt is going to attract hyenas," Darrow noted. "It's 1400 hours now. In another four hours this place will start to come alive."

On a hunch, Akara turned around to see what was behind them on the opposite horizon. He saw movement. "Darrow! Is that a man with some animals?"

Darrow looked through George's binoculars. "Yes, it's a tribesman with a flock of goats. They must have heard the explosion or seen the smoke. If you can climb down off this rock without being in anyone's gunsight you can ask him for help. I see more people and more goats. Good! If they're part of a big encampment they'll probably have a sat phone. If not, one of the kids can run for help. These native kids can really move."

"You're sure they'll speak Portuguese?" Akara asked.

"Of course. Many of them also speak English and Dutch... Not much, but enough to carry on a rudimentary conversation."

"Are you saying I couldn't discuss Leibnitz with them?" Akara joked as he filled an empty whisky bottle with water.

Darrow grinned. "That depends on the quality of your German. While you're discussing philosophy, you might want to be careful where you step," he warned. "There are poisonous snakes down there."

"Snakes? What kind of snakes?"

"Cobras, vipers, adders, boomslangs, mambas... Twenty-one different venomous snakes live in Mozambique. Just watch where you're walking."

Akara had not realized how sheltered his life had been. Most of the fears he had known were personal, intellectual fears... failure to understand a problem or failure to find a solution. He had a natural fear of trusting people who proved to be perfidious and scheming. He dealt with that fear by severely limiting the number of people he trusted. And he also feared unexpected environmental hazards - like floods or lightning thunderstorms or some other unforeseen feature in a landscape. But he was a relative stranger to overt threats by people or hostile creatures. He had hunted before, but he had never been alone. Always he had been in a protective group. He had never been bullied or mugged. He had not played contact sports. And now he was being warned about unknown and overt dangers, and he did not know how to react to them. "What do I do if I come upon a snake?" he asked.

"Stop. Stand very still, and then very slowly and quietly back away."

"I remember reading once," George said, "that Bobby Kennedy went swimming in the Amazon River and his aides were all upset because there were piranha in the water. Bobby kept swimming and called back, 'Whoever heard of a United States Senator being eaten by piranha?' Likewise, my brother, I say, 'Whoever heard of a PhD in Computer Science ever being killed by a spitting cobra?'"

"*I've* never heard of one," Darrow said, smiling. "You're not likely to set a precedent."

George gave him his little knife. "I don't know what good it will be, but maybe you can trade it to one of the kids for his help. It's the same steel Samurai swords are made from. Compounded and honed by hand, and very sharp."

Akara put the knife in his pocket and the bottle inside his shirt front and began to slip and slide on his behind down the far side of the rocky outcrop. Repeatedly he looked back to be sure that there was a monolith between him and the man with the rifle. As he passed one rocky outcrop, he saw a snake coiled on a rock. He had no idea which kind of snake it was but he stopped, stood still, and then slowly backed away. Then he continued to run through the grass in a kind of jumping-jog. In half an hour of stamping through the tall grass he reached the natives.

The leader of the group of goatherds spoke Portuguese and while he did not have a sat phone on him, he said that a couple of kilometers away there was an encampment and a phone was there. Akara left with one of the boys in the group and headed for their camp.

In two hours, a small helicopter appeared in the eastern sky and headed for their position on the rocky outcrop.

"What about those two other men?" Darrow asked.

The pilot was firm. "I'm stretching things just by carrying all three of you. They can make it to your Land Rover with no problem. They'll be safe inside there until I can get a medivac helicopter to pick them up."

"Perfect," said George.

"By the way," Akara said, "the kid who took me to the camp got your knife. He tested the blade and foresaw a million uses for it, none of which involved killing mice."

"On behalf of Mickey and Mighty and all the guys, I am relieved," George said simply as the helicopter lifted off.

The call from Panama City came in to Sensei's room just before noon. The Ambassador himself conveyed the information. "Miss Lee was adamant. She did not want to be returned to China. Evidently she is extremely sensitive about her appearance. There was a well-known Chinese doctor who trained in Hong Kong who now practices in Sydney, Australia. They didn't make a note of his specialty and nobody remembered it. She had multiple medical problems. She was officially released from active duty and, at her request, was flown to Sydney."

"When was this?" Sensei asked.

"What with the international date line confusing things, I'd say that it was on December 28th. We asked for the doctor's name, but they didn't know it or wouldn't give it. Evidently, because of her position as a high-ranking customs' agent, they initially, at least, wanted to limit the people who could have access to her. But time makes most secrets stale. My assistant got the feeling that we were lucky to be given even this much information about her. He didn't press for more. So, I can't speak to the accuracy of the information, but that's what I learned."

Sensei thanked him profusely. He did a quick search of the Sydney, Australia phone directory and found no Sonya Lee listed. He then made a call to a travel website and booked the next flight to Sydney, and for two of the four hours he had to wait until take-off, he paced his hotel room floor, silently chanting.

He was exhausted, and he realized, as the flight attendant came through the aisle, that he had not eaten since he had a few tablespoons of soup in the hotel restaurant and, later, some bread. He ordered a Coke and some peanuts and tried to read one of the books he had purchased in Anchorage.

It was late autumn in Sydney. The weather was nippy and the deciduous trees had lost their leaves, but it was sunny and a good day to be outside.

Sensei sat on his bed and looked through the telephone directory under "physicians" for a Chinese name. There were dozens of them. None would give him any patient information over the phone. After he had spoken to seven receptionists, he gave up and called Beryl. He was apologetic. "I just can't think straight when it comes to Sonny."

"Ok," Beryl said. "If she's still in Sydney, she's not likely to have a driver's license or be able to vote. A visa puts you back trying to interrogate the Chinese or Australian authorities. I can only think of two ways to locate her. Do you have your GPS receiver loaded into your iPhone?"

"Yes."

"Go to an electronics store and purchase a small transmitter and configure it to your receiver and then put it inside a gift of some kind and take it to the Chinese consulate. Explain that you've learned that Former Agent Lee is recuperating there in Sydney and that you don't want to disturb her but you would like her to have a little gift. Show them your passport and other identification. Just sign the gift card, 'From your friends in the Philippines.' Ask if they would they be kind enough to forward it to her."

"That's a great idea. What kind of gift?"

"Let's see. A tea pot that you could put a transmitter up into the spout and put some cotton around it and put a lot of tissue paper in the pot. You'd have to buy the whole set of tea pot and cups. Or, a gift box of various face and hand creams. Scoop out some cream from one of the jars and wrap the transmitter in a little baggie and insert it into the jar. Or, you could go to a fancy doll shop. Plant the transmitter inside the doll. Usually the head is affixed to the body of the doll by a strong rubber band inside it - that's so the head can rotate. You can pull and tilt the head far enough to insert the transmitter, without damaging the doll. Make sure it is wearing beautiful clothing. But since you don't want some clerk to say, 'Hey, this would make a great gift for my kid,' make sure they understand that you're a fellow agent of some kind. Say you worked with her on Adam Chang's case in Tucson, Arizona and the Santa Marta organ donation racket in the Philippines. They will probably have heard of both cases. If they talk to you about the cases, tell them everything you know... assume a shop-talk attitude. They'll deliver it if she's there. If she's no longer there, they may tell you where she's gone... at least in general terms." She thought a moment and added, "They're probably informed about the recent inquiry about her, so there's a chance that they'll seek and find your transmitter; and if they do, there's nothing much they can do to you, but they might arrange to have Sonya moved to a place that is beyond your ability to locate."

"What's the second idea?"

"Go to a Chinese market that has a medicine section and gab with the clerk. Make sure there's no one in line waiting for service and be sure to be buying things. Ask which Chinese doctors who were trained in Hong Kong are now practicing in Sydney and have an international reputation. You'll be asked which specialty you're interested in. Say that your wife was in a car accident. Sonya may need a dermatologist for burns or skin grafts, or an orthopedic specialist for her limb injuries, or even a neurologist because of her concussion and prolonged coma. She may also be getting cosmetic surgery. So just say she's had a variety of injuries and her Australian doctor thinks she should spend a few weeks in a rest home or spiritual retreat; but she won't take his advice because she trusts only Chinese doctors. Inquire about sanitariums that a Chinese lady would like.

"You'll get a few names of doctors and places. Go to another market and repeat the process.

"Remember, it's the beginning of June and she was sent there at the end of December. She won't be in a hospital for five months, and doctors don't make house calls unless they are associated with a specific residential rehab facility where they can go to see a whole bunch of patients at one time.

"Specifying a kind of doctor may not help you as much as just saying one that was trained in Hong Kong which is all you know about him.

"After you've gotten a few place names and a few doctors' names, call the doctors and ask if they send patients there. My guess is that she is suffering more from a loss of identity. She was your beautiful Gong Fu red spike-heeled goddess, and now she's a mess and doesn't want anyone to see her who knew her when she was beautiful. She might be in a rehab center learning how to walk with a prosthetic foot... but this is Sonya we're talking about. She'd have mastered that in a heartbeat. Remember, she doesn't want to be found so she may not be using the name you know her by. Chinese nationals who operate in a foreign area invariably select a first name that is common in the country they're in. She may very well be using her original Chinese name. Do you know it?"

"She was born in Hong Kong to anglicized Chinese. Her real name is Sonya... at least I think it is."

"If that's all you've got, then you have no choice. Try to find the location of a retreat she might be staying in.

Sensei was relieved to have been given direction. He checked the phone directory on his bed table and looked up electronics' stores and Chinese markets. He made a list and left the hotel to check the first name.

At the Sydney Chinese Market he sought out the pharmacist who did not look particularly busy and asked for advice about relaxing herbs. He gave him his American Express card and bought $45.00 worth of plum flowers and ashwagandha drops to put into his tea. "Maybe you can help me," he said. "My wife was in a car accident. She was driving and hit a tree. She got a broken bone, some burns, and a concussion. She will see only a doctor who was trained in China... in particular Hong Kong. Her emotional problems are the worst of them all. I'd like somebody who's got a good reputation. Do you know of anyone?"

"The best in Sydney is expensive but if you're willing to pay, try Dr. Bai. He's a psychiatrist. People come to him from all over. Sometimes he's hard to get an appointment with. If you can't get him try Jeffrey Feng. He's relatively new to Sydney and his English leaves a lot to be desired. Where's you wife from originally?"

"Guang Zhou."

"Good. Both of them speak Cantonese. She'll get along with either of them. Good luck." He turned to help a customer.

Sensei thanked him and went to the next market. The pharmacist was a woman. There were no other customers at her counter and Sensei merely went up to her, smiled, and related his wife's sad story.

"Oh, the poor thing. Does she need 24/7 care?"

"Yes. Just about full time care! And I have to go to the U.S. on business. She should go into a retreat or some kind of rest home for a few months. A good doctor could persuade her. I'm useless, apparently."

"Take her to Dr. Bai... Hu Bai. He was trained in China and he's very well known in Australia and all over the Pacific. What religion is your wife?"

"She's a Zen Buddhist."

"Wonderful! Dr. Bai is associated with several recovery places, but one is definitely a Mahayana Buddhist retreat... The Home of the

Compassionate Guan Yin. It's by the shore. He goes there regularly to see patients. They have a variety of patients there - emotional and also long term physical injuries. While they're recovering they often need the specialized care of the nuns. Many are registered nurses. She'll be in good hands there. Yes, take her to see Dr. Bai."

"Where is this Home of the Compassionate Guan Yin?" he asked.

"Just north of town."

Sensei bought relaxing herbs. He felt like kissing her. Something inside him told him that this was where he would find Sonya. He hurried back to the hotel to call Beryl.

"If you think you know where she is, don't go to the front office and ask for her or try to be clever. She's an important guest in Chinese circles. Did you say that the retreat is by the sea and to the North?"

"Yes."

"Did you Google it?"

"Jesus. No!" He began to fumble with his iPhone. Beryl shouted for him to stop.

"I'm trying to do it now," he said.

"I'm at the console... I can do it better than you." She located an installation that seemed to fit the general description. "Is it sunny there today?"

"Yes... a little nippy but sunny."

"Go to a heliport in the morning and rent a helicopter and get the pilot... here... I'll give you the GPS coordinates."

Sensei scrambled for a paper to write down the coordinates.

"Buy yourself a really good pair of binoculars. Check the outside area. On a sunny morning she's likely to be outside. I truly doubt that Sonya will go with you willingly. You're going to have to take her by force... chloroform her or something. The place seems to be fenced off even out into the ocean. I can't get any more detail than that. But you can by helicopter. Ok. Get the binoculars and hire the helicopter. Call one now for an appointment."

"Ok. But it's too late today to go. I'll call and reserve a pilot and pray that the weather tomorrow is sunny when I ride up there."

FRIDAY, JUNE 14, 2013

Lionel Darrow joined George and Akara for their rooftop breakfast. He was finally prepared to be completely sincere in his accounting of the Jackson debacle. "After Jackson returned from the canned hunt, the police were notified. They raided the recently created habitat, which was on the Mozambique side of the border. They gave a captured kudu to the local tribe and killed two lions, giving the meat and the tails - which are much prized - to the local chief.

"Since Jackson had booked his safari with us, the 'canners' held us responsible for their losses. I had words with one of them in town. I wanted Jackson to get the hell out of here. Frankly I was willing to give him back his money to get him to leave. But the man was determined to recover his Browning. It's a great gun but it wasn't worth what it was costing us in turmoil. Jackson went everywhere looking for his rifle. Sure, after he dropped the lion off at Maudsley's, he could have made an appearance at a pub and then acted more drunk than he was and quietly got a train or plane to Beira or a car ride down. If pressed, I'd have to concede that it was possible that he went down that day and came back the next and just continued to act the fool.

"What bothered me was that he was so willing to pay thousands for the canned lion - and this was on top of what he paid for the safari - *that he showed them how really profitable their criminal enterprise could be*. This encouraged them and they started up again... several times. Each time I helped to get them closed."

"What's the big attraction about going on a lion safari?" Akara asked.

"It's like anything else that requires skill and concentration - plus... plus the element of danger. Golf's a great game that requires skill and concentration, but the ball or the other wild inhabitants of the fairway won't kill you. There are dangerous occupations, but they're not genetically encoded. Many a man who had doubts about his courage and manliness or even his own place in the sun, his existence, has been able to settle those doubts by going on a legitimate hunt. Man's innate nature is predatory. In going out into the bush... with the snakes and the hyenas and creatures that will kill him at a glance... and confronting them and his fears? Is it better for him to squander a fortune on a psychotherapist for years of fifty-minute hours? Really... when a man has realized his innate nature and prevailed, well, you can understand why he wants to put that trophy on the wall. Every time he looks at it he touches a core of stability within himself. Ok. I'll stop preaching."

"There may be another reason, too," Akara said. "When a person is really hunting, he enters a meditative state. It's a spiritual experience. Unfortunately, among sophisticated fools there's a notion that only primitive people establish a rapport with the hunted animal."

Darrow laughed. "Yes... exactly. There's a spiritual aspect to hunting that absolutely nobody wants to talk about." The waiter came to their table to refill their coffee cups. As if to emphasize that no one liked to discuss the spiritual aspects of the hunt, Darrow changed the subject. "I left a report with the police before I came here. The paramedic helicopter couldn't leave until this morning. I hope they arrest them at the hospital and make them pay to get my Land Rover and satphone repaired. I doubt that they'd have Jackson's rifle."

"It's got the initials 'JT' carved into the base of the stock. If you ever come upon the rifle, all we want is a slug fired from it. Maybe you have some ballistic people who can get me a pristine slug that we can use for comparison. Our client wants the proof."

"I see. He just wants to eliminate Jackson. I'll see what I can do, but the gun is probably out of the country by now."

"As I see it," George said, "proving that it was Jackson's gun doesn't prove that Jackson fired the weapon. He could have contracted with someone else to do the job. His friend Tod said that he heard Devers make plans to meet with someone for drinks that day. We don't know if that is a true statement or, if it is, who the person was. It could be a confederate of Jackson's. Maybe by creating such a memorable presence he thought he was giving himself an airtight alibi."

"Maybe..." Darrow echoed, and then began to discuss the weather.

The morning sun shone brightly and filled the helicopter window on Sensei's side with a golden glow that delivered a benediction as they flew north over the edge of the great expanse of ocean that reflected the sky's inordinate blue. He could see rows of eucalyptus trees and felt a kinship to them. They were not deciduous. They would not change with the season. He could hear nothing but the rotor's pulses, the steady beat, like a Roman legion's double-time marching drum.

She has to be there, he thought. In his mind it simply made no sense that she would be anywhere else. It was eleven o'clock in the morning and on such a day as this, he thought, she would be there sitting outside, watching the sea. He remembered the surf at Malibu where they had swum together. Sonya loved shorelines, the meeting place of earth and water. "We'll supply the fire," she had said, "and God will give us air."

The fenced yard of the sanitarium came into view. "You know," the pilot said, "I can't land inside the walls - in case you're thinking about breakin' somebody out."

"No," Sensei answered. "Nothing like that. I just want to reconnoiter the place. I am looking for someone special, but she doesn't know that I'm looking for her. And I doubt that she'd come willingly." He filmed the buildings, especially the chain link fence that extended into the sea. The pilot swung out over the ocean and turned around so that Sensei could use his binoculars to watch a group of women who were sitting in chairs in the middle of a large open area. The doors to the building opened and a woman on crutches came briskly lurching towards them. She showed only her right hand on the crutch handle. On her left side, the axillary support was in her armpit, and the crutch, itself, was held against her body only by her upper arm.

The helicopter passed the point at which Sensei could see her. "Make another pass around," he requested. The helicopter curved over the ocean again and came around to where Sensei could see the woman in his binoculars. She had a dark head scarf that draped loosely around her lower face and neck. At such a distance, Sensei could see no recognizable detail, but he knew that he was looking at Sonya.

The helicopter kept moving. The pilot asked, "Do you want to go around again?"

"No," Sensei said, "we can return now." It was impossible to see anyone's face. Most of the women wore head scarfs or veils like harem girls or had protruding hoods on their capes that put their faces in dark, featureless shadow.

He returned to his hotel room and called Beryl, leaving a voicemail for her to call him back. It was one o'clock in the afternoon in Sydney. It would be eleven o'clock of the previous evening in Philadelphia - or, at least, that was as near as he could calculate. She was probably asleep. Fatigue and frustration overtook him and he fell into a restless sleep.

He awakened at dinner time and got up to stand at the window and stare dumbly at the city lights. His phone was in the charger. It rang and roused him from the stupor. Beryl was returning his call.

"Help me," he begged. "I've got to get someone inside that compound," he said, "and I don't know who or how."

"You don't know what she looks like now. How can you expect someone else to recognize her? If you're thinking that hacking into the hospital system will give you some information, forget it. We'd gain nothing by the attempt. Besides, Akara and George are still away. I don't know when to expect them home, but I'm sure that when they are home, George will be exhausted and Akara will have to catch-up with temple duties. So don't look for any help but what we can come up with ourselves."

"What do you suggest?"

"Try the gift idea and just deliver it yourself to the Guan Yin facility. Mark it for Sonya Lee and leave it at the desk. The only risks you run are that she may see you and then deliberately avoid you, or that she's not using her real name and they won't know who the recipient is supposed to be."

"Ok," Sensei said. "It's worth the risk. What are the odds that she'll be anywhere near the front desk?" he asked rhetorically.

He thanked Beryl and then began to search the phone directory for shops devoted to dolls. He found one that was not too far from the hotel. He also checked to find a good electronics store.

At the doll shop he was confronted with an array of dolls that varied in price from a hundred dollars to a thousand dollars. He asked the clerk if their heads were attached to a rubber band inside the doll.

"Yes," the clerk said warily.

"Could I maybe pull the head aside to put a message inside the head?" he asked.

"Well," she said, alarmed, "not with one that has a porcelain head. No, I wouldn't try to do that if I were you." This eliminated the most expensive dolls from the selection. He did not want to give Sonya any of the cheaper dolls. "I'll be careful," he said, selecting an oriental doll dressed in Chinese silk. It had red shoes on its feet.

"We have a repair service," she said. "Keep that in mind. The head can be replaced... for a price." She was not happy to learn of his intentions.

He bought the transmitter and returned to the hotel. Sitting on the bed, he tried to pull and slide the doll's head enough to insert the device. The first time he grasped the head carefully and pulled it to one side, it cracked. He remained in control of himself. He put the doll and the transmitter into the box and headed back to the doll shop.

"What is this all about?" the clerk asked as Sensei put the broken doll on the counter. "Don't tell me you were trying to slip a note in there. What are you up to?"

Sensei looked so sheepish and ashamed that she hoped he wouldn't start to cry. He placed the transmitter on the counter. "The woman I love was injured in an explosion at sea. She lost an arm and a foot and suffered burns. Here..." he opened his wallet and his iPhone and showed her photographs of him and Sonya together. She is ashamed of the way she looks and won't let anyone see her. I love her and I don't care what she looks like. I can't live without her." His eyes brimmed with tears until one spilled down his cheek. "I wanted to locate her with this GPS device."

"Well, why didn't you say so? Men! They always have to complicate things." She went into the rear of the shop and returned with a porcelain doll's head and a strange hooking device. "Is this thing on?" she asked, picking up the transmitter.

Sensei indicated that it was on. She reached for some cotton batting. "I'm going to stuff cotton around it in the head or else it will rattle around. Will that affect the transmission?"

"No."

She hooked the interior band to the head and presented him with the doll. "I'll only charge you for the head and, Lord knows, that will be enough to teach you a lesson. Don't try to be clever and outsmart a woman who knows her business. You won't succeed." She gift-wrapped the box, put the box into a fancy bag, and gave him several blank gift cards. "Here!" she said. "Be upfront about it!"

"Yes, Ma'am. I'll be direct from here on in."

Outside the shop, he filled in Sonya's name on the envelope and left the interior of the card blank. Then he hailed a cab and asked to be driven to The Home of the Compassionate Guan Yin.

In Beira, George and Akara wanted to interview the local witness who saw Devers Thompson when he returned from his fishing trip with Gordon. At the police station they asked where they could find one Luis Mulanga.

"He has a fishing boat and should be coming in soon at Pier 4. He doesn't know any more now than he says he did then. He said he saw Gordon and the large fat man leave port and return. They were gone an hour or so. He saw Devers Thompson climb the boarding ladder and get back on board the big moored sailing ship."

"What about Joao Magaia, the longshoreman who repeated the rumor that Jackson had gone on a canned hunt?"

"He moved up north to where his wife was from. He's been gone half a year at least."

Akara thanked him and said they'd be off to Pier 4 and for the record, they'd probably spend the night in Beira and take the morning flight down to Maputo to check in again with Colonel Eusebio Machel.

Luis Mulanga had just docked his fishing boat at Pier 4. In a rustic Portuguese that Akara barely understood, he immediately insisted that he had no knowledge whatsoever about Gordon Thompson's escape. All he would confirm was that he saw the early return of the fat father and the thin son.

Akara wanted to take his photograph, and with George standing beside him, Luis Mulanga posed for the camera.

It was late afternoon and no one was sitting outdoors in the seaside garden. Sensei asked the cab to wait, and then he climbed the front steps of the retreat, opened the glass door, and went into the large reception area. Immediately, he stopped walking. The room was central to several large, pie-shaped facilities: a dining room that was filled with people opened directly into it. Nearly everyone in the dining room could see him. On the other side, a recreation and therapy room similarly had him completely in view of the few people who were in the facility. A hallway, behind the receptionist's desk, led to the second floor stairway and to the patients' rooms that were situated on the first floor.

Sensei put the gift box up to the side of his face to shield it from the many eyes in the dining room that were able to see him. He quickly did an about-face and left by the same door that he had entered.

Ominously, as he returned to the hotel, intending to sit calmly as he discussed the situation with Beryl, dark clouds had rolled in from the south and it had begun to rain. "How long do you think this will last?" he asked the cab driver.

"We're good for a couple of days," he said.

By "good" Sensei understood him to mean that rain was good for cab drivers. It was not good for abductions.

"I can't do it," Sensei confessed to Beryl. "I don't mind going in there and taking her out by force... but that will have to be done at night when she's sleeping and there is only a skeleton staff on duty. I can't go in during the day when she can see me and hide. What can I do?"

Beryl thought. "You need someone to get that doll to her... to place it in her hand or leave it in her room. You could try hiring a P.I. down there or you could ask a favor of someone up here... someone who doesn't mind long flights and is personally fond of you. I'm thinking that Sylvia Maitlin might agree to help you. She knows enough Chinese to get by. I can email the head of the Home and ask if she would mind if a nun from our order visited the facility. I'll think up some religious group and program it into our all purpose phone and email address. I can compliment her on the reputation for excellence that the Home enjoys and say we'd like to get some guidance for a similar facility we want to create. Sylvia's got the guts to pull off an entry into the complex, masquerading as a nun from a religious order."

"No... not Sylvia. Sonya knows what she looks like and would also know she's associated with me! What about Lilyanne? She knows how to act like a nun... pray like a nun... dress like a nun... Would she do this for me?"

"Oh, my God. Sylvia is at least in Seattle. You'd be asking someone to fly from the east coast all the way to Australia just on the chance that she could deliver a doll. It's crazy! Do I think she would do it if you asked her? Yes, I think she would. But I warn you! *George cannot find out about this.* Remember! You don't know what kind of enemies Sonya had that put her in the ocean off Attu. You cannot let George know you're enlisting

Lilyanne's help in something that could be dangerous for her. He acts like he doesn't care what happens to her, but if he thinks you put her in harm's way, that sleeping giant in him will wake up and squash you. But ask her. The worst she can do is to say, 'No.'"

"Will you ask her for me?"

"No, Sensei. This has to come from you. I have her trust and I don't want to lose it. I don't want her to think, 'What's she after now?' every time I call her. Besides, George would kill me if I got involved."

"All right. I'll call her."

Beryl sighed. "Let me know what she says."

Lilyanne Smith had just finished giving Baby Eric his morning bottle or, more accurately, the day nurse had just finished giving him his bottle. "Bath time," she was still cooing as she answered the phone. Sensei explained in tearful detail all that had happened.

"What is it that you want me to do?" she asked.

"I believe that I saw Sonya sitting in the garden at the sanitarium. But I'm not absolutely certain. I know enough to know that in my state of mind I'm likely to see what I want to see. I have nothing else to rely on but my gut feeling. So what I'd like is for you to dress up like a nun and to verify that it is Sonya I saw, sitting in the garden there at the Guan Yin House." He explained Beryl's suggestion about a letter of introduction.

"But you said this was a Buddhist sanitarium."

"It is. But you could go as a nun who is interested in starting a similar retreat."

"I wouldn't go in a nun's habit. Sensei, for heaven's sake! I'm a former novice who's in good standing with her religious order. I don't have the right to do that. On the other hand, I've often thought about creating a retreat. We have many abandoned old houses around here. I could convert one into a retreat. All right. As a religious businesswoman, I'll go. But I cannot stay long. What do I do when I encounter her? I've never met the woman. How would I know her when I see her? Sensei, have you thought this through to its logical conclusion."

It had not been so very long ago that Sensei was lecturing Lilyanne on the necessity to think a course of action through to its logical conclusion and to consider all of the possible consequences. And now his pupil was cautioning him to think before he acted. "I have a GPS transmitter inside a gift and you'll have to find a way to locate her and to give her the gift. Then I'll be able to locate her at night and take her out of there."

"Kidnap her?"

"She's my woman."

"And what if she doesn't want to go?"

"She loves me. She'll want to be with me."

"Even though she hasn't contacted you since last September?"

"Look! Do you want to help me or not? I know what I'm doing. I just don't know how to do what I'm doing."

"Well," Lilyanne said trying not to sound sarcastic, "in that case I'll come immediately. I'll call you back with my flight information."

"Wait!" Sensei said. "I forgot to ask Beryl if we could use her passport for Sonny. I'll engage a private jet to fly us out of the country, but they may want to see a passport. Could you pick it up and bring it with you?"

"I'll call Beryl and ask. If she's willing, I'll pick it up myself. With all of you dumping all your duties on her, I'm sure she doesn't have the time to drop it off here at Tarleton. Incidentally, I will be traveling as Lilyanne Haffner. Beryl's letter to the directress will have to refer to me in that name. Wait there until I call you back."

Sensei had heard nothing about Lilyanne's name-change. He knew her baby had been named Haffner, but that was all he knew. He also wondered how Lilyanne knew that George and Akara were out of the office. "She must be in some kind of regular contact with Beryl," he correctly thought. "Nobody tells me anything!"

An hour later Lily called to tell him her Quantas flight would land at 8 a.m. Monday morning at Kingsford Smith International Airport.

SATURDAY, JUNE 15, 2013

George and Akara checked-in with Eusebio Machel. They made sure they had their plane reservations fixed so that they could have an easy way to break free of any conversation that got too close to the truth.

"What did you discover in Manica?" Machel asked.

"We spoke to the taxidermist who is losing business to the freeze-drying places. Evidently it takes months to freeze-dry an animal."

"Why should that be?" Machel asked.

"Mammals are composed mostly of water," Akara replied. "The first thing they do is to freeze the animal. The water becomes ice, then the dehydration process begins. The ice must be directly converted to gas - like water vapor in the air - without going through a liquid stage. Anybody can heat ice and make it liquid water and boil it until it becomes steam. But that's not what freeze-drying does. Through chemicals and pressure the ice is converted directly to vapor in a vacuum chamber and expelled; and the specimen is dehydrated perfectly. Depending on the size, to do it right may take many months in a dehydration chamber. This is an oversimplification, of course. But it takes capital to get started. We think we know some people who may be interested in investing in such an enterprise in Chimoio."

Machel had recalled the photographs of Akara and George dressed in evening clothes in the residence of the rich Mr. Thompson. He was much more interested in the industrial development of his country than in the guilt or innocence of two brothers. Nevertheless, there was still the business of a half-open criminal case and a body that had incurred considerable expense. "I've spoken to Charles Thompson and found him to be an agreeable fellow... very pleasant. Unfortunately, the fees for the cremation and the recovery and the legal fees still haven't been decided. The situation was so unusual. There is no routine procedure that anyone can follow."

"Yes," George said, "It's a unique case. But perhaps if everything else is cleared up, when the initial consultations are made about the freeze-dry facility, Charles or Gordon or their representatives can attend to the transfer of the remains of Devers Thompson."

"If the case is dropped," Machel said encouragingly, "then I suppose all the expenses related to the case would be paid by the deceased's family. That would be normal anywhere. No?"

"Indeed," George said. He stood and indicated to Akara that it was time to go. He patted his shirt pocket from which his airline ticket protruded. Akara warmly shook Machel's hand. "You'll be seeing us again, I hope," he said.

Machel nodded. "I truly hope so. Let me have my car take you to the airport."

They arrived in plenty of time to take the flight to Johannesburg. Once there, they checked into a hotel, dressed and dined, and prepared to take their trans-Atlantic flight in the morning.

MONDAY, JUNE 17, 2013

Sensei awoke Monday morning and rushed to the window to check the weather. He sighed with relief to see the shining sun. This was a good omen, he thought. He hurried to the airport.

Finally, the jetway was put into place and the first class passengers came into the gate, Lilyanne Smith Haffner among them. Sensei hugged her. "Did you bring any luggage?"

"No. I'm traveling light. I cannot stay long. I do have Beryl's passport and I'll see the project through, but then I really do have to get back."

"I understand."

At the hotel, Lilyanne checked into the room she had reserved, showered and changed her clothes, and went to Sensei's room to discuss the details.

He reviewed the layout of the place by showing her the videos he had taken and as he remembered it. "At a sunny time of day, she'll probably be in the gardens that are on the sea-side. So try to get a tour of that area. He gave her the doll with the red shoes. "There's a GPS transmitter inside the head. I'll be able to find her tonight with the signal."

"Beryl sent them an email letter of introduction, saying that I'd be there probably this afternoon. She wrote as Sister Marie Claire, Mother Superior of a religious order that had heard many nice things about The Home of the Compassionate Guan Yin. She wanted me to look the facility over and meet some of the staff and patients, too, if they were agreeable to it, to use merely for reference. She told them I was a former Catholic novice. Beryl says that I'm to tell them the truth about myself... about my convent life... that I can afford to renovate an old mansion for the purpose, etcetera, etcetera."

She called the Quan Yin Home and, after exchanging greetings with the Directress, made an appointment for 2 p.m. that afternoon to visit the facility.

Lilyanne rented a car, and after lunch she went with Sensei to the Guan Yin Home. She carried the doll, which was a gift from Sister Marie Claire for any patient who looked like she would appreciate it. She would suppose that Sister Marie Claire thought that there might be little girls in the facility.

The Directress, Shi Fa Lian, had verified Lilyanne's mission with the Mother Superior of the Order of Saint Luke the Physician. "Welcome, Ms. Haffner," the Directress smiled and said. "I spoke to Sister Marie Claire who said some very nice things about you." She looked at the fancy bag Lilyanne was carrying, but her visitor made no attempt to give it to her or even to explain its existence.

They began to chat as Lilyanne received the guided tour. "And your view of the sea that I've heard so much about?" Lilyanne said, hoping to see it.

They exited the building and walked towards a group of hooded or partially veiled women who sat in the sun. "The veils are to protect the face from the sun... burns or scar tissue," the directress explained.

Lilyanne had never met Sonya Lee but she recognized her immediately. She could see only her eyes beneath the scarf that covered her head and the lower half of her face; but what was more revealing was that Sonya's right hand was gracefully formed into various gestures as she spoke and that she was missing a left foot and hand. Sensei was known to rave about the graceful movements of Sonya's hands.

Lilyanne stopped to talk to the women. Directing her remarks specifically to Sonya, she asked, "Will this be your first winter 'down under'?"

"Yes. I hear it's not so bad. Windy, perhaps."

"I was asked by Sister Marie Claire to give someone a gift. Am I correct in assuming that you're Chinese?"

"Yes," Sonya said. "Born and bred."

Lilyanne handed Sonya the decorative store bag that contained the boxed doll. "I hope you enjoy it," she said. "It's a pretty Chinese doll. I hope you don't find this awkward. I think Sister assumed there would be little girls here. But you seem to be sufficiently young-at-heart."

Sonya opened the box. "It's a beautiful doll," she said. "I'll cherish it always. And she's wearing red shoes! They're my favorite. Thank you and please convey my thanks to Sister Marie Claire."

Sensei was watching the GPS readout when Lilyanne returned to the car. "Did you see her?"

"Yes. I gave her the doll. She seems to have her wits about her. She admired its red shoes. I don't think she suspected that it came from you."

"How does she look? Healthy?"

"Her face was mostly covered because they don't want the sun on any burned area; but other than that, she was speaking to a few women as I approached and she spoke rationally to me. When she looked up I could see both of her eyes. I asked her if this would be her first winter 'down under.'"

"Thank God!" Sensei sighed. "My greatest fear was that she was suffering with brain damage from the disaster at sea. Well, I've bought hospital scrubs and tonight I'm going to break into the retreat - it shouldn't be difficult - and follow the GPS beacon. I'm going to take her. I'll probably need a gag. I'll use a nylon scarf. She'll fight me. You just keep the motor running out here and be ready to roll." He got out his phone. "Right now I'm verifying the appointment I made for private jet service. Tonight we'll be on our way home. Let's go to the hotel and have something to eat and then check out. You drive. I want to see where she's going."

At 9 p.m. while Lilyanne waited in the car outside, Sensei, dressed in a physician's scrubs, turned on his iPhone and followed the transmitter's beacon. He guessed that Sonya's foot injury would probably keep her on the ground floor of the two-storey facility, and as he followed the beacon, he was led to her room on the first floor. She was already asleep. A little crinkled paper pill cup was beside her bed with a half-empty glass of water. At the side of the room stood a folded wheelchair. Sensei opened the chair, slipped a gag across Sonya's mouth and tied it behind her head. He scooped her out of the bed and sat her in the wheelchair before she roused herself. He grabbed the doll that was lying on the pillow beside her, put it on her lap, and walked to the entrance. In a clear voice he said, "If I show you the evening stars, do you promise to go to bed and stay there?" He smiled at the receptionist who stared at him suspiciously.

He lifted Sonya out of the chair, descended the steps, and pushed her into the rear seat of the sedan as he jumped in and shut the door. Lilyanne stepped on the accelerator. She could see the receptionist standing on the steps as she turned onto the highway.

"Head for the airport!" Sensei said jubilantly. "We leave at eleven."

Sonya was groggy and only vaguely aware of what was happening. "Uugh," she said repeatedly, trying to say, "No" through the gag. "Uugh" she tried to hide her face. He took the gag out of her mouth.

Lilyanne expected a maudlin scene as Sensei whined to Sonya about how much he loved her and missed her. Instead, he was furious.

To Sonya's repeated, "No!" Sensei countered, "Yes!" He grabbed her shoulders. "Now you just shut your mouth! How did you dare do this to me?"

Lilyanne raised her eyebrows but said nothing. She headed for the Executive airport.

"No," Sonya wept. "Take me back. I will not be seen like this. Please... have mercy! Take me back."

"I ought to slap you silly," Sensei shouted. "If I had any sense I'd beat you to a pulp. How could you do this to me? What kind of man did you think I was that you could just abandon me? Did you think I was some asshole businessman who screws his secretary because his wife gained twenty pounds? An idiot who needs a trophy wife to bolster his ego? Is that what you thought of me? Is it? *Is it?* How could you leave me in such torment for all these months? You wait until I get you home," he snarled, "Agent Lee. And you are going home! You are going home with me where you belong. And another thing! We're getting married. Like it or not!" A weepiness crept into his voice. "Do you know how you've hurt me?" He gulped and his voice cracked. "And if you give me any shit, I'm gonna kick your ass, Gungfussy."

"Oh, Percy, I am so sorry!" Sonya said, sobbing. "My Ka-ra-te Man! Forgive me!" She began to weep uncontrollably. Suddenly she stopped crying and looked up at him. "*Gungfussy*? You never called me that before." She turned into his arms.

Lilyanne ceased looking into the rear view mirror.

In his temple office-bedroom, Akara Chatree was finally able to read the Local Usage Details of Jackson Thompson's phone. He could readily see ordinary calls and patterns of traffic between numbers that were of pre-paid "burner" phones. "Is it safe to assume these 'burner' numbers are of phones used by drug dealers?" he asked George who was standing behind him, looking over his shoulder.

"There's no guarantee that they are," George replied, "but in fact drug dealers usually do use those pre-paid phones. They change them every week."

"Jackson was also apparently being dunned for past due bills. He communicated with half a dozen collection agencies. Obviously, he was in financial trouble and, judging from the phone traffic, it must have been serious trouble. Norma Beckridge gave me her number, and I see it's down here," he counted, "four times in one month. That doesn't sound like much for a dating game. But these anonymous burner phones? If we can't run down the owners by any records, wouldn't it help to tail him? I'm assuming they're not delivering drugs to him at his home. If I had a prepaid phone, I'd call them myself; but I don't want to use my own equipment."

"If Charles Thompson is willing, we can plant spyware in Jackson's phone. I'll call and ask." George called the client who was not inclined to spy on Jackson.

"I know what the boy is doing," Thompson said. "And I saw the two thugs who came to the house that day. Wiretapping his phone isn't going to be admissible in court, and I don't want him to say that what I did was no different in terms of sleaziness than what he did. Let's keep it honest."

George agreed. He then returned to the office while Akara continued to look over the phone records. Something about the bill was wrong. As he began to study it, the Temple door's buzzer sounded. People were arriving for services. He rushed to his closet and put on his uniform and robe and descended the stairs two at a time to open the temple doors.

Charles Thompson was waiting in Beryl's front office for George to arrive.

George entered through the rear door and, seeing Thompson's parked car, knew that his client was there. "Charles!" he called. "I haven't had time to write up the case. Take a seat in my office." As George went to speak to him in his office, Beryl went into the rear utility kitchen to make coffee.

"Well," George said, "we found out some interesting information about the lion hanging in your den. Do you know what they call high-end cars when they're traded in and resold?"

"You mean a 'used car'?" Thompson replied.

"The euphemism is 'a pre-owned car.' The lion that Jackson bought was owned by another fellow. It was, in a sense, a 'pre-hunted lion.'"

"Oh, no! A canned hunt! Colonel Machel indicated that Jackson had shot the lion in the bush... 'a lucky shot,' he said."

"I'm afraid that Colonel Machel wishes that were the case. It isn't. The lion was probably born in a petting zoo and then, when it grew up and was too big to pet, it was sold to a park that kept it in a cage until a hunter wanted to kill a lion. And then it was let loose in a fenced area and the hunter, in this case Jackson, shot it. Or rather, shot at it. His bullet grazed its flank. The man who owned the canned hunt facility apparently killed the animal."

"No wonder Jackson was able to get back so quickly. That gives Jackson all the time he needed to con my brother off the ship and kill him."

"In my opinion, he did not do it. Sure, he could have worked fast. He made such a complete ass of himself before the hunt that everybody remembers him. And there is no verification of his presence for the whole of that first day. Everyone says he became drunk and belligerent after he dropped the lion off, but that could have been faked. He had claimed that someone stole his rifle and went all over looking for it. So, yes, between moving around and acting so outrageously he could have established an alibi.

"It takes half an hour to fly from Chimoio to Beira. A little disguise and who would recognize him? Two and a half hours to drive. The taxidermist was definite about the time that the lion was delivered to him. It was 11 a.m. He could have gone out to the ship which was moored - not docked at the shore - and killed his father and tossed his body overboard. Remember, it was raining that day. There was an afternoon thunder storm. The crack of lightning or thunder clap could have masked the sound of the shot. The current there is so strong that the body would have traveled a great distance all on its own. He wouldn't even have to take out a fishing boat. All this is conjecture.

"It was undoubtedly Jackson who supplied the authorities in Maputo with a Portuguese copy of the will, making sure they understood that Gordon would inherit a fortune upon his father's death. Gordon found a $1400 charge on a house-use credit card statement. We checked it out. It was for a Portuguese translation, not an Italian one that Jackson had claimed."

"I'm confused. Then you do think it was Jackson who murdered my brother?"

"No! I don't think that at all. I can only eliminate someone who couldn't have done it. He could have. It's just my opinion that such an action would require the character of a bold and confident man. Before the safari began Jackson proved himself to be a weakling, a pawn. He behaved with such dramatic cowardice when he was confronted by an old toothless lion that no professional hunter would go into the bush with him. He had jumped up onto a table, spilling ammunition as he tried to load his rifle."

"But if he could put on such an act - and acting and being 'on stage performing' is certainly in character for him - why couldn't that fuss he made over the old lion have been an act too?"

"Because he also shit his pants. Not even Richard Burbage could have crapped on cue."

Charles sighed. "Then you think he conspired with Tod?"

"No. I think Jackson owed some rough people a lot of money, and the sooner Devers died, the sooner they'd get their money. But who, in his right mind, would conspire with Jackson? A conspiracy is a partnership. A conspiracy to commit murder is a life and death partnership. Would you bet your life that Jackson Thompson would perfectly execute his half of the criminal activity?"

TUESDAY, JUNE 18, 2013

The private jet landed at the executive area of Seattle's SeaTac airport. Since Sonya had no viable passport, it was necessary for her to call her old friends at the Chinese consulate in Seattle and to request a replacement passport. She emailed them a photo to use and the attaché who met the jet in the executive terminal was able to deliver a completed passport. Terrell Maitlin, Sylvia's husband, had been a former police commissioner. Through his connections he obtained the "medical emergency" visa stamp.

The reunion was joyous yet, when the attaché saw Sensei carry his old friend down the jet's short stairway and Lilyanne carry Sonya's crutches and adjust her scarf, he burst out crying and hugged her, telling her in whispered Chinese that he had thought she was dead because she had been injured so seriously. He turned to Sensei, "You're getting my dear friend all the care she needs?"

"You can rest assured," Sensei said. "I'll start getting that care while we're here in Seattle."

Sonya had been upset about having to face people she didn't know in Philadelphia. "Not where you live, Percy," she had pleaded. "I'm not ready for that."

She was, however, willing to see Sylvia Maitlin. Sensei called first while Sonya slept and explained the situation. "Bring her here immediately," Sylvia ordered. "And you say that Ms. Smith Haffner has to get back to her baby? Ok. If she can't get suitable accommodations bring her with you, too."

When Sonya had awakened, she was relieved to learn that she'd be staying with her "sister" friend Sylvia. It was Sylvia who waited with open arms for her to clear customs. The two women cried for five minutes and then went to see Lilyanne off on the good connections she was able to obtain on a commercial flight.

At the Maitlin's home, Sonya was surprised to see that Sylvia had converted what once had been her living room and porcelain gallery into a bedroom for Sonya and Sensei.

"What happened to all your beautiful Chinese porcelains?" Sonya asked.

"I split them up between a few museums back east. People around here don't appreciate porcelain properly. Let me rephrase that. People around here don't appreciate *my* knowledge of porcelain properly. I have a new hobby. I've joined a gun club and have already competed. I won my class division first time out. If I practice every day diligently for ten years, maybe I'll be as good as my hero... you!"

Sonya showed her the doll. "Percy got this for me. Red shoes. I should have known."

"Well, we'll get you a pair of spike red heels... just as soon as we get you fitted for a prosthetic foot and hand."

"They're very expensive," Sonya said. "My government would fit me with them if I agreed to go home. So I've learned to get along without them. Up until yesterday, it didn't matter."

Sylvia Maitlin took charge of Sonya the way she had always taken charge of everything in her life. She called a wig shop and asked the store owner to come to the house with an assortment of wigs. "Hold on," she said and called to Sonya, "Black hair, short with bangs? Curls?"

"No curls. Bobbed and bangs is fine." The owner heard Sonya's response.

"Bring only your best," Sylvia said. "In an hour? Fine." Then she checked the internet for prosthetic devices and the doctors who fitted them. "Girl, ain't no moss gonna grow on you. Tomorrow when you've got hair and makeup on, we can have a look at feet that fit in red spike heels... but you'll probably need platform soles to start with."

"Good!" Sonya replied. "Once I get my foot, I'll be able to test my balance at the gun range."

Sylvia gasped. "I have dreamed of this moment! We'll have a regular shoot-out!"

As Beryl and George sat in his office working on the official reports of the case progress, the office phone rang. Beryl answered. "Just a minute," she said, handing the phone to George.

Colonel Eusebio Machel spoke boldly. "I have good and bad news, Wagner. I did some digging for you.

"First, the good news. There is a thousand kilometers between Mozambique and Madagascar and I suggested to the attorney who is prosecuting the case that we really do not know whether Devers was killed in international waters and that Mozambique may not have jurisdiction in the case at all. Naturally, Gordon should be fined for breaking out of jail, but he can probably afford the fine."

George raised his eyebrows and signaled a thumb's up to Beryl.

"Now the not-so-good news. As you know," Machel continued, "I'm more interested in the construction project. I took a ride out there myself and did some investigating. If the information I got is accurate, Jackson had his rifle when he went to shoot the lion. But none of the safari guides knew what happened to it after that. I went back to Maudsley and got the name of the man who pushed the cart. Miguel. He told me that Jackson mistakenly left the Browning in the Land Rover when the dead lion was dropped off at his house. He said that Jackson was determined to get the rifle back. He contradicted me about the location of the shoot. He said that Jackson made quite a fuss about being taken back to a habitat... a habitat *in Zimbabwe*... but nobody wanted to go there. It occurs to me that if he were eager to get back to Beira to kill his father, he wouldn't have given a damn about his rifle - as excellent a rifle as it was."

George said that he agreed with him. "Yes, if that was the case, it doesn't make sense that Jackson would have delayed his return."

"I was hoping to have better news for you, news that would have exonerated his brother. I can only tell you that if Gordon Thompson shows up here, he'll probably have to pay a fine. Finally, after Jackson picked up the lion's head on the afternoon of the 4th, he still didn't have his gun, so he rented space in a restaurant refrigerator to put the box that contains the head... which is mostly hair so the box is not that large. He found his original guide who denied knowing anything about a rifle or an illegal hunt. Jackson thinks that he can pry information out of someone with a little gin, which is why he was already drunk when he got the call about his father's death. He missed the train back so he had a few more drinks and wound up drunk and getting dumped into some fleabag hotel. He slept nearly the entire day of the 5th, and couldn't start back to Beira until the morning of the 6th. He might be fined, too, for going in and out of Zimbabwe on that illegal hunt."

George thanked him for the information. "It's helpful, but not necessarily as bad as we might suppose," he said ambiguously. "I'll call you back if I hear anything more. As soon as the problem's resolved, Gordon Thompson wants to proceed with the freeze-dry facility. He may need a good local architect. So if you know one, give him a head's up. He'll also want to take care of those outstanding recovery and funereal expenses. Let us know as soon as the fee is determined."

The Colonel said that he hoped George and Akara would attend the opening of the facility and George said that they wouldn't miss it, "for a million bucks."

Beryl waited expectantly to hear details of the news. "Jackson's time *after* the murder is pretty much accounted for. I guess since he was never considered a suspect, nobody bothered much to check him out. They don't want to call attention to the canned hunt. As far as Devers' death is concerned, Jackson didn't do anything on his own or with an accomplice. It never happened that way.

"On the other hand, it is possible that Tod took it on himself to do away with Devers. This would mean that he and Jackson were really tight. If Tod did it on his own, he would have to be sure he'd benefit when the inheritance was given to Jackson. He'd have control over Jackson.

So how tight are they? Are they lovers? For Jackson automatically to overlook Tod's potential guilt and to blame his own brother, he either prejudicially believes Tod's story about the argument or else Tod's got something big he's holding over Jackson's head and Jackson doesn't dare even to voice the possibility that Gordon is innocent."

WEDNESDAY, JUNE 19, 2013

Everyone associated with the case agreed to meet in the den of the Thompson home at 10 a.m.

While George and Akara, and Charles, Gordon, Jackson, and their attorneys sat in a large circle of stuffed couches and chairs, George began by stating that Colonel Machel had raised the question of jurisdiction. "The body of Devers Thompson may have been located in international waters. Of course there are fines to be paid for escaping from their jail. The smart thing at this point is to have Gordon's attorney go to participate in the discussion of jurisdiction and to pay those fines immediately. Machel is more interested in the new freeze-dry plant which Akara very wisely promised to build himself or, as he put it, 'Let Gordon Thompson have the honor.'" As Gordon suddenly raised his eyebrows in surprise, George said, "We'll get back to that later.

"We need first to settle the matter of the canned lion hunt. This is an issue that is driving the events more than a simple act of one tourist murdering another. The proof of the canned hunt is still held by the taxidermist, Maudsley.

"Maudsley also can testify that on the first day of the hunt, September 3rd, Jackson's whereabouts could be accounted for only up until the time he dropped the lion off at the taxidermist at 11 a.m. or noon, although," he added, "in that call from Colonel Machel I was told that he, Machel, had done some investigating and learned that Jackson did create quite a stir trying to get a ride back to the canned hunt operation in order to find his rifle."

Jackson got up and stood under the lion. "This is an outrage. I shot this animal in the wild and anyone who says otherwise is a liar."

His attorney, Bradford Douglass, asked Jackson to please let him do the job he was being paid to do. "Please do not speak... just sit down and be quiet!"

Jackson sat down. "First of all," Douglass said to George, "you have no way of knowing whether the carcass you saw was ever attached to that lion's head. It could have been another lion. Nothing is changed by your investigation."

Akara countered, "A DNA test of the carcass and the head will establish that they are the same animal. Freeze drying does not destroy DNA. And there's always the dentine in the teeth. There was evidence of a bullet grazing the lion's flank but the bullet that brought him down was of a bigger caliber. That slug is preserved in the taxidermist's shop." He showed him the photographs he had taken in the big refrigerator.

Jackson ignored his attorney's advice and stood up again, petulantly. "When you are on Safari," he said with a smarmy tone and expression, "more than one hunter may find it expedient to shoot at an animal. And a single hunter may elect to use two different guns. As it happened, I used a larger caliber weapon which I rented. Because of my father's preference for the Browning, I just didn't want to make the Browning seem less significant by saying that I didn't use it. And as far as finding sausage in the animal's stomach, who is to say that the big cat didn't attack campers before I encountered him? No, I'm afraid that your DNA test will prove nothing. What you *are* trying to do is to blame me for killing my father, and I did not kill my father!"

Douglass sighed and stood as if to wrap things up. "I don't know what your mission accomplished. You can try to produce witnesses, but they won't be considered reliable. After all, the same people you will want to use to prove Jackson's guilt are the same people who came forward to prove Gordon's guilt."

Charles Thompson looked at George. "Has all this been for naught?"

Akara answered. "No, of course not. Call a laboratory and have them send a technician here to pull several hairs out of the lion's mane. If the cat were always in the wild an analysis of his hair will not show the chemical additives that preserve food. Sausages and other foodstuffs that humans consume are full of preservatives: benzoates, nitrites, sulphites, sorbates. The lions used in canned hunts are usually fed slop from restaurants or meat products that are too old to sell. The animals were caged long enough to absorb these chemicals into their hair. Let's conduct the test shall we? Between a hair analysis and a DNA comparison, plus the testimony of witnesses who were not interviewed in preparation for Gordon's trial - the guides, cooks, Safari officials, taxidermist, plus the men who ran the illegal lion compound - we ought to make a compelling case for Jackson's deceit."

Douglass objected. "Even if you prove that the lion was killed in this manner, you will have to manufacture evidence if you want to claim that Jackson killed Devers Thompson; and isn't that what the case is really about?"

Charles Thompson countered. "Let me remind you that I can disqualify Jackson on moral grounds. And if we can prove that he has lied so cleverly about this lion and further, that he used his behavior in Chimoio to establish a memorable alibi while he engaged a confederate to kill my brother, he will automatically be disqualified. If you're so certain that he's innocent, perhaps you should return to Mozambique with him to establish his innocence. My brother worked hard to earn his money and I don't think he intended that I give it to someone who would simply squander it sinfully. I have many aspects of Jackson's conduct to consider... drugs, gambling, this lion fraud, and also the disposition of the inheritance his mother left him. If he shows that he has invested is inheritance wisely, I'll consider that an offsetting merit." He turned to Jackson. "Can you produce those bonds or show what you've invested the money in?"

Jackson could not control his contempt. "Who the hell are you to ask me to account for anything that's mine?" he demanded to know. "I am under no obligation to show you anything!"

"And I am under no obligation to allow you even to live in this house. In fact, the more I think about it, the more inclined I am to think you need to move out of here. Yes, you have thirty days to clear out. I will make formal application for your eviction immediately." He pointed to Gordon. "Call a laboratory and have them come and take DNA samples and hair shaft samples of that... that trophy to Shame." He signaled his own attorney. "Move ahead immediately with closing all of Jackson's credit lines to which this estate is co-signatory." His attorney took out his phone and called his office and told his secretary to proceed with the credit cancellations.

Gordon's attorney, Marvin Abrams, stood up. "I for one am interested in these test results." He looked at Gordon. "Let's get that call made immediately to an accredited laboratory."

"What does it matter how I shot that lion?" Jackson squealed. "It still doesn't mean I killed my father!"

"Let me put it this way, Jackson," Charles Thompson said. "You will not get a penny of my brother's money until I get satisfactory answers and some proof that you are not a complete wastrel."

"I owe people money!" Jackson shouted. "Do you want to have me killed over some non-payment of debts?"

"Since you've inherited that money, you've done nothing but engage in a program of self-destruction. I am not going to assist you in killing yourself. Stop living the life-style you've been wallowing in and work something out with your creditors."

"They'll kill me - but that's what you want! But don't worry! They'll kill you first since you're the only obstacle between me and the money due me. You and my traitor brother!"

George looked out the window. Two police cars and one unmarked vehicle pulled onto the driveway. "Why are the police here?" he asked.

Charles started to walk to the front door. "They're conducting a search for drugs. I've given permission but they also have a warrant. It seems Jackson has been on the DEA's 'watch list' for months. They weren't too happy about all the lion publicity coming before they were ready, but I wanted to be here when they searched." The houseboy had already opened the front door. "Come in, Gentlemen," Charles called. Jackson tried to run to his bedroom, but he was grabbed by Charles who immediately turned him over to a uniformed police officer.

Akara called Gordon aside. "I've been swamped with work since we got back. I apologize. I should have mentioned the freeze-dry facility. I promised Mr. Maudsley, the taxidermist, that you or I would build it. If you don't care to do it, don't worry about it."

"Of course I'll do it. Did you make any provisions for the two men who helped me escape?"

"No. I have their names, though. I guess you'll have to do that... after the charges against you are dropped."

"I'll send my lawyer over there first. I wouldn't want to walk into a trap. Listen," he said with a definite hope, "if I do go to Mozambique, would you consider accompanying me?"

"It's ok with me. We'll have to run it past the boss." He nodded towards George.

The warrant specified that the police could search only Jackson's bedroom, bathroom and car. One of the plainclothes detectives spoke to his counterpart who was conducting a simultaneous raid on Tod Beckridge's apartment. He whistled. "We were told these guys were distributors. I figured small time stuff. Jackson's got some cocaine and heroin. We'll have to have them tested to determine how strong they are. But the quantities are still small... enough to arrest him for possession - but not enough for an intent to sell."

Tod had significantly larger quantities hidden in his house. They agreed to keep Jackson and Tod separated when they were brought into the Delaware County lockup.

Charles Thompson was visibly distressed to see Jackson taken away with his hands cuffed behind him. Bradford Douglass tried to console his client. "I'll have you out in no time. Say nothing to no one."

Thompson looked grave. "I am supposing that you will be bailing him out, Mr. Douglass. As much as it pains me to say it, I will not be." He turned to Gordon. "And you?"

Gordon looked at his pleading brother. "Jacky, for God's sake. You tried to have me convicted of murdering Dad. Don't come looking to me for help. Personally, I think that being in custody is the best thing that could happen to you now."

As Akara and George drove down the driveway in the bright red Corvette, they noticed a Lincoln parked on the highway near the estate's entrance. George read the license number aloud and kept repeating it until he could write it in his notebook. "There were two guys sitting in the front," he said. "I didn't get a good look at them because I wanted to get the plates."

"I know, so I looked. Middle aged, thick necked, one bald and one with grey wavy hair. I'm guessing from the broad chests and double chins that they were both fat dudes. They looked Latin, to me. More indigenous Mexican than anything else. Colombians and Brazilians seem to be fairer. But I'm bi-racial. I can never pick out racial characteristics definitively."

"Call Charles when you get back to the temple and describe them to him. Maybe they're the thugs who scared Devers into taking an ocean trip last year. I'll call Charles now about getting a bodyguard." He placed the call.

Charles Thompson was not inclined to hire a protector. "My nephew is trying to scare me into submission. I will continue to live my life exactly as I have been."

George shook his head. "Two thugs were parked down in the street. Akara will call you and describe them to you when we get home. Maybe they're the same ones you saw before. Meanwhile, let me know if you change your mind about getting a bodyguard. I think you should give it some serious thought."

The case was far from over.

Court had adjourned for the day. The pair would be arraigned the following morning. The county "jailhouse" physician was called in to examine both Tod and an increasingly erratic Jackson Thompson. In the few hours the doctor required to arrive at the jail, Jackson began to exhibit withdrawal symptoms. Despite being ordered by his attorney to say nothing, he could not keep quiet. He began to accuse every one of conspiring against him. The physician recorded that he had found him to be "irrationally fearful to the point of paranoia, irritable, and showing signs of incipient formication." Jackson's manicured fingernails were longer than the usual length, and he had begun to scratch long red lines into his arms. "He may need to be hospitalized," the doctor said, "but for now the jailhouse infirmary will do. He's been medicated."

He noted that Tod was asymptomatic and exhibited no abnormal distress. His nasal mucosa showed no sign of drug use and his vital signs were all normal. Psychologically he was calm and rational.

Without comment, Tod Beckridge signed papers and gave blood, hair, and urine samples for testing. The technician who took his prints thought that he exhibited a slight and understandable nervousness, but no excessive stress.

Charles Thompson had called the detective who had supervised the search. "They'll both probably be arraigned tomorrow morning at the courthouse," the detective said.

"Will they both face the same charges?"

"Beckridge is not a user. He claims that he was holding the drugs for Jackson who purchased them. We've pulled his phone records and there's no indication that he was a dealer, though he may have been a party animal who distributed drugs to his rich friends. Beckridge had student loans to pay off and he says that Jackson paid him to hold the stuff and to help him try to curtail his habit by judiciously giving him the drugs when he absolutely needed them. That's how he was able to meet his loan payments. He also has a job and helps to support his family. He's got no arrest record, whereas... your nephew has been arrested a few times."

"I didn't know that!" Charles said.

"He never did any prison time... but he was jailed for DUI and failure to pay traffic citations and for having small amounts of drugs on his person. Things will go harder for him."

Charles Thompson called George and asked if he and Akara would accompany him to the courthouse the following morning.

"Can I have a raincheck?" Akara joked. "I've got a date tonight with Norma and I naturally cannot tell you when I'll be back."

"Or *if*..." Charles said.

Half an hour before Akara would have started to drive to her residence, Norma called to tell him that she wanted to be taken to the last purely nouvelle cuisine restaurant in the area. "A friend of mine owns it and I'd like us to make a noteworthy entrance."

"Does that mean 'formal'?" he asked.

"Yes. I have a new gown I'd like to wear."

"Would you prefer me to wear a white dinner jacket or a black one?"

"You look wonderful in black. And since my dress is a champagne color, black would be better. But what is a Zen Buddhist priest doing with so many formal garments?"

"I get invited to awards' banquets. I helped write a few papers with colleagues in my academic life. I'll pick you up shortly."

At the restaurant, she began to question him, circling around the topic that Akara knew was central to the discussion: the future of Jackson's inheritance.

She asked, "Do you think Charles could force Jackson to return to Mozambique?"

"I don't think that it's in the man's nature to force someone to do anything. Did Devers ever force you to do anything?"

"Sexually? I was fifteen years old. By definition, whatever we did was done by his use of force."

"Legally, no doubt. But a young tigress doesn't care that she's an endangered species, that it is illegal to hunt her. She'll taunt the hunter, killing his gun-bearer while the fellow sleeps."

"And you think I, as a teenaged virgin, baited a trap for Devers?"

"No. You're not the type. You have a funny kind of independence. Frankly, I admire it. You probably simply came to a meeting of the minds. I know real diamonds when I see them, and those earrings and that necklace and bracelet are real. Did Devers give them to you?"

"Yes. You *are* perceptive! But, since you asked... It started with his wife's jewelry," she said, laughing. "Already I'm telling you my life history." She hesitated for a moment. "Well, why not? Let's see... ten years ago. Devers' wife had recently died and all his friends and associates were trying to match him with one of their relatives. One night Tod and I came to the house to see the boys, and D came home early from what was supposed to be a business dinner, but was just another match-making attempt. That angered him. He came up to his room to change his clothes and found me sitting at his wife's vanity trying on the same earrings that I wore the other night. I had pinned my hair up. He walked in and instead of my saying, 'Oh, I'm so sorry!' I looked right at him and said, 'I always admired these on Mrs. Thompson, but they look good on me too.' He pulled off his tie, hung up his jacket, and tossed his shirt studs into a dish on his dresser. As he took off his shirt, he said, 'There's a necklace that goes with the earrings. He unlocked a cabinet and took out a velvet box. He opened it and tossed me the necklace, saying, 'Give me a minute and I'll put it on you.' He stripped and stood behind me. I was wearing a cotton blouse that had a high mandarin neck. So I removed my blouse and bra and I reached up and behind me and made little clawing marks on his waist as he put the necklace on me. The pose must have suggested bondage to him. He told me I was now his caged beauty and he tossed me onto his bed and that was the start of the affair."

"It doesn't exactly sound like rape," Akara said, "statutory or otherwise."

"I told Tod to call home and say that we were spending the night. D was like a bear... ferocious one minute and cuddly the next. In the morning he took a ruby broach out of the cabinet and said, 'Here, you were great last night.' I said, 'Ugh. It's ugly. Put it back.'

"'It's valuable,' he said. I said, 'I don't care how valuable it is. I don't like it.' And then I handed him the necklace and the earrings that were tumbled in the bed linens. 'These I like,' I said, 'but put them away, too.'"

"How long did it continue?"

"From the summer of 2003 to the fall of 2006. I adored him and I think I'm not being vain when I say that he absolutely adored me. Sexually, he was marvelously relentless. I immediately told my parents that because money was so tight at home - my father had lost a considerable sum - that I refused to go to private school and needed to enroll in a local public high school. Then I made Devers buy one of those windowless vans so that he could come by my school at lunch time. I could never have gotten off campus in prep school. I never had any girlfriends at school... nobody to report me. I couldn't get enough of him.

"We planned to get married as soon as I turned eighteen in November 2006. We had our reservations made. We'd fly to Las Vegas and come back as man and wife, *fait accompli.* A couple of weeks before my birthday we went hunting near Harrisburg and he accidentally stepped into an animal trap. It stressed him terribly... the pain, the surgeries, and the drugs. He already had high blood pressure but he gained weight from inactivity and all that comfort food, then he started to take medication for his blood pressure and he couldn't even get an erection any more. He changed towards me. I had been spending so much time with him that my parents sold our house and took a small apartment for themselves. Tod got his own place. And then one day Devers put a bunch of jewelry in a bag and gave it to me, saying that I should get a life for myself. So I moved in with Tod. But I loved the man that he was in that portrait. I loved him so much. I miss him and our hunting trips." She sighed. "Do you go?"

"In Brazil, in the Pantanal, I went with my mother's relatives. And a couple of times in Minnesota I went hunting with colleagues of mine who needed to get away from Academia for a few weeks. We never killed a creature we couldn't or wouldn't eat."

"I'm glad to hear you speak well of it. People who disapprove of hunting usually suppose that the leather in their shoes and the steak on their plates came from cows that committed suicide. It's odd, though, thinking about a Buddhist priest hunting."

"I've known priests who were pedophiles. That's even odder. Man is a born hunter, and he can remain pure in the hunt. There's no such thing as a pure pedophile. I sometimes think that in no other spiritual environment can you develop the depth of meditation that you can attain in hunting. The concentration is truly one-pointed. Your collective unconscious takes over and you get into an *uber*-zone. You can go without water, without sleep, without food. You're not trekking, you're stalking... transfixed on the prey. It's as if your Buddha Self takes over.

You anticipate with a kind of sixth sense. You have a spiritual connection to the event and to the prey. It's an incredibly soulful experience."

"Oh!" she said. "You'll have to take me hunting someday."

"But you have Jackson to take you. Don't you regularly go out with him?"

"Not locally."

"Where then?"

"Atlantic City. He gambles a lot and calls me when he needs more cash or coke. Make love to me tonight." She used the same tone she would have used to say, "Pass me the salt."

Akara gulped. Once again, he did not know how to respond to a woman's bold remark.

"It's a mistake to equate love with sex."

"It was just a figure of speech. Have sex with me tonight."

"Sure," he said. "Where?"

"In my apartment."

"I thought you lived with your brother."

"I do. But I have my own private entrance."

"No. I would not be comfortable."

"I know of a charming inn you'll love, if I may use that word without disturbing your vocabulary. They serve breakfasts that you'll also love."

"I can't stay all night."

"When will you have to leave?"

"I open the temple at 6 a.m. You'll have to be ready by 5 a.m., or else I can give you cab fare."

He did not care which option she chose. He had learned much of what he needed to know.

THURSDAY, JUNE 20, 2013

Lilyanne Smith called Beryl. "How bad are Sonya's injuries?" Beryl asked.

"A hot pipe or part of a boiler fell across the left side of her face. She's scarred. It's about three inches wide and runs from her neck up her cheek and ear and the side of her head. Part of her hairline is gone. Fortunately, it missed her eye. She must have been in a section of the boat that was intact and floating, although it was full of water. When the hot metal hit her, it didn't get a chance to burn deeply... at least that's what they told her. The cold salt water neutralized the heat. Maybe the thing remained buoyant beside her. There must be some reason she didn't get any frostbite... none at all. She lost her left foot and lower left arm because they had been crushed in the explosion - not because of frostbite. There was nothing they could do to save her arm and foot. And Sonya has no recollection of anything. She can't even remember why she was on the ship in the first place. The two men who were floating with her had been killed when the ship blew up."

"How long was she in the water?"

"About ten minutes, she was told. The Coast guard was tailing the fishing boat. They must have known something illegal was going on; but they're not talking and Sonny can't remember. The last recollection she has is knowing that she was supposed to go to Kushiro, Japan. She doesn't know why she was supposed to go there. So, that's it. Blessed oblivion."

"How is she mentally?"

"Seventh heaven. Sensei and Sonya are inseparable. He has never been so happy. He told me that if you took every happy moment he had experienced in his entire life and packed it into one hour and put that hour next to any hour of being with Sonya, there would be no contest. He's really ecstatic. So is she."

"But that burned-off section of scalp? I'm wondering if she can find a tissue match. How big a piece would she need to replace the burned hair area?"

"I'm guessing... Two inches by four inches. The long measurement is the vertical one. She wouldn't need the hair from a corpse... a living person could part with that much scalp... I mean, if the hair was thick... from the back of the head someplace." Lilyanne's tone changed suddenly. "You're not thinking about calling that Carla person?"

"Well... she's the one who knows all about organ transplantation and skin is an organ."

"There are thousands of people in this world who know about transplants. I see no reason why you would even consider contacting her about any of this. If you intended to bring her into the affair, you should have left me out of it!"

"Lilyanne! There is no love triangle between you, Carla and George. The person we want to help is Sonya Lee. I really wish that you and George would stop putting me in the middle. The moment one of you gets mentioned, the other shuts down the conversation."

A moment passed before Lilyanne whispered, "I'm sorry. All right. I admit it. I'm jealous of her. And if he wants to parade her around in front of me in the cause of helping Sonya, well... never mind. Forget I said anything. If you can, come by for breakfast tomorrow morning. 8 a.m. We'll be expecting you. Tell 'You Know Who' that Sensei and Sonya will be my house guests. Akara can run the temple by himself and 'You Know Who' can manage your office. It won't kill him to do a little office work."

Beryl took a deep breath. "Love," she said to herself, "is the same the world over."

Tod Beckridge had been willing to use the services of a public defendant, but Charles Thompson, after learning that Tod had been trying so valiantly to wean Jackson away from his drug use, secured for him the services of a young lawyer, Angela Saracco, who had a good reputation for defending drug cases. Charles had assured her that it was, "the least my family can do to compensate this young man for his efforts on Jackson's behalf."

Tod and Angela Saracco were waiting in the courtroom for Jackson Thompson and Bradford Douglass to arrive.

Charles, Gordon, and George were waiting, too, as they sat in the rear row of seats. Charles stood and motioned to Tod's attorney to come back to them for a moment.

"You wanted to see me?" she said as she approached.

"What charges will Tod be facing?" Charles asked.

"At the moment, only possession."

"Is he going to testify against Jackson?"

"I can't answer that. He's said publicly that Jackson had no control over himself whenever he had a drug supply at his disposal. He started to use so frequently that Tod became alarmed and asked him to let him hold the drugs for him so that he could put the brakes on his drug use. He sort of rationed them and did get Jackson to cut back. Naturally, the D.A. wants to know where Jackson purchased the drugs. He's probably willing to deal for that information, but Tod says that he didn't know and that he didn't *want* to know. Other than that he says that Jackson is his friend and has been so for years. He seems ready to take responsibility for his own actions. He told me, 'I know I placed myself and my family in jeopardy by trying to play a rehab doctor; but Jackson refused to enter treatment, and I didn't know what else to do.' We certainly have no plans for him to testify against Jackson. Tod doesn't have anything to give them."

"What are his prospects for bail?"

She shrugged. "His mom and dad are in the courtroom. They've already told me that anything more than token bail will be out of the question for them. But Tod's resigned to remain in jail until the trial."

Jackson, his attorney, and a bailiff entered the courtroom. "I think that they just brought Jackson here from the infirmary," Saracco said. "From the looks of him, they'll be taking him back there, too."

"We can't let Tod stay in jail. Doesn't he have a job?" Charles asked.

"Not any more. His father just got a call from his employer. He was summarily fired for being 'involved' with drugs."

"Tell them not to worry. I'll pay his bail. I hope that doesn't embarrass his family. His father was an old fraternity brother of mine. We used to play golf together years ago. Can we keep my part anonymous?"

"There's really no point in trying to keep your generosity a secret. You'll have to sign..."

"Well, don't disclose it if you can avoid it. Just say, 'a friend paid the bail' if you're asked."

Jackson and Tod were both charged with possession, but Jackson's case was continued, pending further medical reports. Tod Beckridge was free on a $200,000 bond. As Charles went to arrange for payment, Gordon and George went outside the courthouse and stood on the steps.

"Will you continue to run down the facts?" Gordon asked.

"Yes. We still haven't solved the murder."

"I've asked Akara to accompany me to Maputo," Gordon said quietly, "if that's all right with you." Akara had not mentioned this to George previously. Gordon quickly added, "I'll need his language abilities in order to get the promised freeze-dry facility started and to help the two men who saved me. Mainly, I want to pick up my dad's ashes. I could really use Akara. I'd feel safer with him there."

"He's a little expensive to use as a bodyguard or a translator," George said, "and for the record, both Maudsley, the taxidermist, and the man who runs things, Colonel Eusebio Machel, both speak English. Why don't you send your attorney over to get the charges dropped and pay your fines and bills before you do anything else. Frankly, Akara's religious duties alone would be enough to keep him here. He's officiating without any help at the temple right now and he'll continue to be alone for another month, at least."

"I just didn't want to seem like a scared rabbit, hiding in a burrow somewhere waiting for a chance to run. I wanted to get this over with." He saw his attorney, Marvin Abrams, begin to climb the courthouse steps. "I've asked Abrams to come so that I could make some intelligent plans." He signaled his attorney.

George continued to suggest a plan that didn't involve Akara. "Then since you've got to stop in Johannesburg anyway, stay there. Maputo is only two hundred miles away. You can video conference, and when your attorney gets the charges officially dropped, you can go to Mozambique and get your dad's ashes and pay your bills, and then you can shake Machel's hand personally and also talk to an architect."

Abrams had listened to the plan. "I think we've got enough to get everything but the fees dismissed. The plan is workable. I can clear my calendar for the next week, so if you want to go sooner than later, let's get the show on the road."

"I'm free anytime," Gordon said, taking out his phone. "I welcome the chance to get away from all this craziness. If your passport's in order, we can get an online tourist visa and leave tomorrow. If not, we can always get the visa in Johannesburg."

"My passport's in order," Abrams said. He waited while Gordon booked two business tickets on a morning flight to Johannesburg with next day connections to Maputo for one person. "I'll meet you at the KLM desk at 7 a.m."

George said that if they wished, he would call Colonel Machel to let him know they were on their way.

"Yes," said Abrams, "by all means, call and announce us."

"Well," Charles Thompson said with finality as he re-joined the group, "that ends that. I'm free now to move that rascal out of the house and to go to the Poconos to oversee the summer camp set-up and interview personnel."

Tod Beckridge came down the courthouse steps with Bradford Douglass and Angela Saracco. He thanked Charles and signaled his parents to wait a minute. "Let me know if there's anything I can do to help. News of our arrest was all over the papers, and apparently, I've already lost my job."

"I'll hire you right now to help me get Jackson's things moved out of the house and to help select an apartment to put his things in. They'll probably put him into some medical probationary program. I want him to have a residence within walking distance of a treatment facility. After we do that, I'll hire you to accompany me to the Poconos. You'll still be inside the Commonwealth of Pennsylvania."

Bradford Douglass held a hand up, indicating that he wanted to slow down the sequence. "That's a bit premature, Charles. Can I ask you to postpone moving any of Jackson's things from his bedroom? It will go easier for the boy if the judge thinks he's got a legitimate home to go to. I'm not asking you to forgive anything he's done, I'm just asking that you not do anything to make things worse for him."

Charles agreed. "Tod!" he exclaimed. "If you want a job, meet me at the house tomorrow morning at 8 a.m. and we'll get that summer camp project taken care of."

"With pleasure!" Tod replied. "See you at 8 a.m. *Mañana.*"

Akara sat at his computers looking for answers to questions that were nagging him. Something was missing and he had to find it. Sensei's absence had placed the responsibility for the temple on him... all the Dharma talks that had to be written... and the chants that had to be recited... and there were forms for everything that he still wasn't sure he had learned properly... the different ways to hold the incense as he offered it... how to form his hands into the correct mudras. And of course, he had to be available for counseling the sangha members. It was this last duty that gave him the most anxiety. He had had no idea that so many people called the temple to discuss their personal problems. When he complained to Beryl she said, "Akara, in the land of the blind, the one-eyed man is king. Go and rule!"

And then, of course, he had to make room in his schedule for the beautiful and probably lethal Norma.

With very little time to consider the problem cogently, Akara reasoned that Jackson wouldn't be gambling in Atlantic City alone. He'd be with Tod. And, since Norma lived with Tod, she had ready access to the drugs and the cash. Furthermore, since the hour's drive to Atlantic City probably stretched to the limit of the time anybody could reasonably wait for more drugs or money to gamble, she had to answer the summons immediately. This wasn't some kind of favor she was doing for him. No, it was a job. No doubt, Jackson could get no more credit from the casinos or from any drug dealer. This meant that Norma was an employee; and the story about Jackson being her escort had no romantic basis. Friend or lover, Tod was the one who spent the most time with Jackson. In support of this supposition was the noticeable fact that when Jackson called Norma for drugs, he did not call any of the other "burner" phone numbers.

But something was wrong. Who were all these other people Jackson called?

Sensei called Beryl to report on Sonya's progress. "She's been fitted for a prosthetic foot. She actually got to try a model on and, just as you said, immediately she was almost to the point where you cannot tell the difference. We pick hers up this afternoon. She's getting a non-mechanical prosthetic hand. She absolutely does not want a mechanical hand. If she changes her mind we can get the problem solved locally. Now, the wedding." He paused to take a deep breath.

"Sylvia Maitlin wanted to hold our wedding at her house here in Seattle. But Sonny knows that all my friends are back with you guys, so she declined. As soon as Lilyanne heard this, she offered to have the ceremony at Tarleton. It's so beautiful there, especially at this time of year. Sylvia will be coming to be Sonny's Maid of Honor and I'll be asking George to be my Best Man. What do you think?"

Beryl wanted to say, "George would rather be poked in the eye with a sharp stick than set foot on Tarleton soil," but she quickly replied, "He would be honored."

While they were speaking George came into the office. "Who would be honored?"

She said to Sensei, "George just arrived. You can ask him, yourself." She handed the phone to George and watched him as he listened to Sensei's request.

"Well, Congratulations, old Buddy," he said. "I can hear the joy in your voice. And of course I'd be honored. Will I need a morning frock coat? Something in grey and pink? A top hat?" He paused. "Evening? Better yet. June 26th. Perfect. Yep. That's me. The Best Man."

He hung up the office phone and looked sternly at Beryl. "Did you set this up?" he asked.

"I only wish I had. Is there no end to your adolescent idiocy?"

FRIDAY, JUNE 21, 2013

Promptly at 8 a.m., Tod Beckridge knocked on the Thompson house door with his left hand. His right hand and arm were in a sling.

"What happened to your arm?" Charles asked. "Anything serious?"

"No. You know that old joke about the guy who steps on a rake and the handle flies up and hits him in the head? Well, I did just that only the handle whacked me on my clavicle and I got some kind of bone bruising - if you can bruise a bone! I'm glad we're not moving furniture today. Other than that the sling should be off by tomorrow."

Thompson touched Tod's good shoulder. "Good, let's get moving. The most important thing is hiring the right people for the camp. I want complete background checks. I hope you have your portable computer with you."

"I do, indeed!" Tod said as they walked together to the garage.

Akara Chatree munched on day-old pizza and tried to compose the evening's Dharma talk. But Jackson's mysterious phone record would not vacate his mind. Everything was happening so fast that he never seemed to find the time to think constructively. He had to be overlooking something that was obvious. But what? There were phone calls from Atlantic City to Norma Beckridge and now he knew what they were all about. But the unknown numbers? Were these for drugs or some other vice?

He went to an electronics store and purchased a prepaid cellphone. At the temple, he began to call the unknown numbers. They were all disconnected. What was he missing?

He thought about Sherlock Holmes. *Silver Blaze*. How did it go? As best as Akara could remember the story, a police officer asks Holmes if there is anything specific he wants to know about the stolen racehorse, *Silver Blaze*. Holmes says that there is. He is interested in the actions of the guard dog on the night that the horse was stolen from the stables. The officer replies, "The dog didn't do anything on that night." And Holmes says, "That is the action I'm interested in." Suddenly Akara knew what was missing. He shouted, "It's not what did happen, it's what didn't happen! There were only a few land-line phone calls from Jackson to Tod locally. If the person who was stealing *Silver Blaze* had been a stranger, the dog would have barked. If Jackson had called his best friend Tod, Tod's number should be on the bill. It wasn't." Akara swatted his forehead. "You idiot!" he shouted at himself. "The pre-paid phones belonged to Tod!" He picked up the phone bill and ran down the street.

Akara burst into the office, yelling, "I figured it out!"

"I'm happy for you," George said. "What did you figure out?"

"Remember these disposable phones? There were only a few regular calls to Tod from Jackson. Those disposable numbers had to be Tod's. He's got Jackson's drugs. He may sell to others, but there's no direct phone link to him because of the prepaid phones. Norma's the conduit... the mule. Jackson did call her from Atlantic City where he had to be with Tod. And when he was with Tod, there were no calls placed to disposable numbers... just to Norma.

"Norma has access to Jackson's money and his drugs. She admitted that when he called her it was for her to deliver more money or drugs to him. 'Cash or coke,' she said.

"I figure that Tod wanted a marriage between Norma and Jackson. But she wouldn't marry him unless he already had the money. I think he killed Devers to bring about the inheritance. And then Jackson inherited the million in bonds from his mother and Tod wormed his way into becoming Jackson's drug and gambling buddy and probably got to use some of that money to fund his own drug business. But again, as with the canned hunt, Jackson became a problem. At the rate he was going through cash and was morally and mentally deteriorating, Tod would be desperate to have Jackson inherit his father's money before he completely fell apart or before Charles officially cut him off. So far, what do you think?"

"Sounds right to me," George said. "Which is why Charles should get himself a bodyguard. But I'm past the point in my life when I try to coerce people into acting in their own best interest. The man likes Tod and trusts him. Charles is a fool."

Akara persisted with his theory. "But getting rid of Charles might not completely solve Tod's problem. Jackson would get the money; but by then his mental state might be too erratic and unreliable. What would Tod do if Jackson decided that there was no great reason for him to marry Norma? After all the loving care Tod has given this project, he's not going to let it go down the drain so easily. He would need insurance that he could get his hands on Jackson's money. If marrying Norma wasn't in the cards, then he'd have to find something to hold over Jackson's head."

George was surprised and proud of Akara. "Yes! And that adds weight to the suspicion we've had. Good work! This means–" George said, letting Akara finish the line.

"That if Tod already has that 'blackmailing thing' he doesn't have to wait around for a more opportune time to get rid of Charles. In fact–"

"He might find it better to act immediately - that is to say, before Jackson was convicted of a crime. Do we have any indication... any suspicion by anyone that Jackson could have done something that Tod's using against him?" George thought for a moment. "It's too late to ask Gordon, but maybe you can get Norma to tell you something."

"No. She's part of the scheme and she'll protect it like a lioness protects her cubs. Norma is a totally self-absorbed person. Half-person. Quarter-person. She's not really all there. I look at her and think about what happens when an animal's caught in a trap. It either gnaws its foot off or it starves to death. Before the trap accident, she and Devers must have been one great couple... a unit. Afterwards, the unit dissolved and she was left alone to starve to death."

"I don't know how much good it will do to try to warn Charles, but since he's going to be with Tod up in the mountains, we ought to at least try to put him on guard." George got out his phone. "If they're on the road right now, I'll ask him to turn back. No sense taking any chances."

Akara jumped up. "I'll get the Corvette out of the garage. We may need to pursue them."

Because of Tod's shoulder injury, Charles Thompson had insisted on driving his old Cadillac. By noon they were leaving Highway 476 and were turning right onto Highway 81, heading for Stroudsburg.

Tod unbuckled his seat belt. "I can't take it any more," he complained. "This seat-belt harness is really making my shoulder uncomfortable. I'm not worried. You're a safe driver. The road ahead curves in and out and up and down as it goes through the mountains."

"You know this road?" Charles asked, surprised that Tod hadn't mentioned this before.

"Sure. I went to summer camp, too. And, for the record, I loved it."

Charles' phone rang. Still holding the wheel with his left hand, he put the phone to his right ear. He recognized the caller. "Yes, Wagner."

George lowered his voice. "This is urgent. Do not say anything. Just answer my question. Are you driving?"

"Yes."

"Is Tod sitting on your right?"

"Yes."

"Put your phone up to your other ear."

Thompson switched hands. "Ok."

"We have good reason to believe that Tod killed Devers. Jackson probably knew nothing about it. We figure that Tod may pull some kind of stunt to get you to plunge off the side of a mountain road and then jump out as you're going over the edge... or something equally deadly. I'm asking you as strenuously as I can to stop driving with him. You are in danger. Can you stop at a restaurant?"

"Sure. I'm getting hungry right now. It's lunch time."

"Drive slower. Do you know the name of a restaurant nearby?"

"The best Shoo Fly Pie east of Lancaster can be gotten up ahead at a little place called 'Schmidt's Tavern and Grill' right at the Warrenburg Highway junction. I need a rest and unfortunately my assistant has an injured arm and can't spell me. But I'm gonna treat him to some Shoo Fly Pie and maybe even a steak for lunch."

"We're on our way. Charles, do not continue to drive with him. His arm injury is probably faked."

"Yes, I can see that possibility clearly. Just like in the movies. Well, you tell her I said that's wonderful. I wish her the best of luck. See you soon."

George regretted that he couldn't drive a manual transmission any more. The Corvette took the turns and hugged the highway even better, he had to admit, than his Porsche did. Akara was in complete focussed control of the vehicle. George observed his maneuvering skills. "This car is showing off," he said.

Akara did not answer. "Hey!" George yelled. "Do you have that iPad thing with you?"

"Yes."

"When we get to where we're going, you have to connect to that stack of gizmos you've got at the temple and find out what the hell Tod Beckridge has on Jackson Thompson. His current drug habits are not enough. Are they lovers? Tod dominates Jackson. You need to find out about their past together. Maybe Jackson did something bad that Tod knows about and nobody else knows. Sex tapes... something."

"So now I'm a magician?" Akara arched his eyebrows and glanced at George.

"Yes. Keep your eyes on the road."

Tod and Charles were still working on dessert when the red sports car pulled into the parking lot. George entered the restaurant first.

"I'm sure glad we got to you as soon as we did. You've got to get back. Jackson tried to kill himself. They've got him in a psych ward."

"Why didn't they call us?" Tod asked.

"Because Jackson begged them not to. He told them to call us, and here we are. I didn't want to tell Mr. Thompson such bad news while he was behind the wheel. Tell me, is that car you're driving an automatic shift?"

"Yes," Charles said.

"Good," George replied. "Then I'll drive your car back and Tod can ride with Akara in the Corvette."

As soon as they returned to the highway, George called Bradford Douglass. "We've figured out that Tod Beckridge is the one who killed Devers Thompson. My own opinion is that Jackson didn't know anything about it and that Tod is counting on Jackson's support because Tod's got something, possibly sexual, possibly criminal, that he's holding over Jackson's head. My guy is trying to find out what that is. So talk to your client and try to get him to tell you about it. If it's just some embarrassing cause for blackmail, you handle it. If it isn't, we'll need police participation and have Jackson wear a wire and discuss Devers' murder with Tod.

"There was a bunch of disposable phone numbers listed on Jackson's LUDs. We've got good reason to believe that those numbers belonged to Tod. That man is not the innocent and helpful friend he pretends to be."

Bradford Douglass did not want Jackson involved in the murder. "I need to be reassured that this isn't an effort to deflect attention away from Gordon."

"It isn't. Charles Thompson's life is the one that's in danger now." George outlined the events that had brought them back from the Pocono Mountains. "We used the fiction that Jackson tried to kill himself. So go along with it. No matter what Jackson's done in the past, he won't be in the kind of trouble he'll be in if Tod turns on him to save his own ass. Charles will bear the cost of defending Jackson for whatever it was that Tod's got on him." He looked at Thompson for confirmation.

"Whatever it takes. You can count on it."

George and Charles Thompson, and Akara and Tod drove directly to the Delaware County jail. Bradford Douglass and Charles' attorney were there to meet them. "How is Jack," Tod asked.

"He's holding on, but he's still critical," Douglass answered, signaling a police investigator who immediately approached.

"Let's have a look at that injured arm of yours," the officer said. "We've got an orthopedic specialist inside."

"Thanks, but that's not necessary. It's healing on its own."

"I insist. After he examines you, we'd like to ask you a few questions. We don't want someone to say we hurt a suspect during an interrogation."

"I want to see my attorney," Tod protested.

His attorney was called. While they waited, Douglass went into the infirmary to speak to Jackson.

Half an hour later, Douglass returned. "He says he'll talk to the guy who knows the Internet - if he really is a priest."

"I'm fully ordained," Akara said, "and I guess I'm the guy who knows the net."

George wished that he could see Akara in action. The young priest entered the infirmary and pulled up a chair beside the bed to which Jackson was shackled. "How are you feeling?" Akara asked.

"Better. They've got me on some cocaine withdrawal medication. Is everything we say privileged?"

"Yes." Akara did not, in fact, know whether or not privilege did apply since Jackson was not a member of his temple sangha. He reassured Jackson. "Nothing you tell me will be used to harm you in any way. You have my word."

"What's going on? Nobody will tell me anything. Why am I being asked to turn on Tod?"

"Because Tod has been behind all your troubles. Ok. Two things happened. When I examined your telephone records, I found out that Tod had all the disposable phones listed on your phone bill."

"How did you find that out? He disconnected all of them."

"At first I figured they were calls to your dealer. But they came in a pattern. When you were in Atlantic City with Tod, you didn't make any calls to a disposable number. A few of those times you did call Norma. But something didn't add up on your phone bills... something was missing and I couldn't see what it was. Then I remembered a Sherlock Holmes' story called *Silver Blaze*. A thief steals a horse from a stable, but the guard dog doesn't bark, so Holmes realizes that the thief was not a stranger. The dog knew him. Then it occurred to me that with a couple of exceptions, you made no calls to Tod. Calls to your best friend were missing. Obviously, those unknown numbers were his.

"Around the same time I flashed to that, George got a call from Colonel Machel in Maputo. He learned that you had started looking for your Browning right after you dropped the lion off at Maudsley's. You were so determined to get your rifle back that he figured if you intended to sneak back to the ship and kill your dad, you wouldn't have wasted time looking for a rifle and getting drunk."

"A lot George Wagner cares about my innocence. He made a fool out of me."

"He was just trying to solve a murder. It got complicated because Colonel Machel doesn't want any bad publicity about canned hunts. George and I already figured that you did have time to get back, but that you weren't the type to kill anybody. You'd have needed Tod's help. But Tod is too smart to entrust you with being a partner in crime. You've become an addict. I'm sorry if that offends you, but that's the fact. Tod neither needed nor wanted your help. He's pulling the strings here. And you need to tell us why he is able to do that. Your uncle will support you with any help you need. Tod is going to turn on you... trust me."

Jackson became defensive. He angrily dismissed Akara's estimation of Tod's character. "Don't try to drive a wedge between us. He's been my best friend for years. I know in my heart that he would never turn on me. He'd risk his own life to save mine."

"Jackson, that is sentimental bullshit. Let me explain something to you. Friends and enemies are like a two-sided coin. It's the instinct of self-preservation that 'shadows' our interactions with other people. It tells us who is our friend and will be beneficial to us and who is our enemy and will be detrimental to us. And it's often wrong.

"You talk about Tod as though he were the friend John speaks of in the Bible: 'Greater love hath no man than this, that a man lay down his life for his friends.' John is speaking about another instinct entirely: the Hero. Tod is no hero.

"Real fears about self-preservation will convert a friend into an enemy in an instant. Think about the 'coin' verbs they use in criminal law. Two friends commit a crime and are caught. The prosecutor separates them and says, 'Whoever first rats out the other one will get the better deal.' He says that he 'flips' one and gets him 'to turn' state's evidence. Tod is gonna turn on you. He's already started."

"Tod won't let me down. My brother and my uncle are the reason I'm chained to this bed."

"Your use of drugs got you chained to this bed. Tod's after your money and he intends to get it one way or another. And then your life won't be worth one of the links in that chain."

"And just who is worried about my life? Tod's the only one who has ever given a damn about me."

"Try thinking about the events of the past year from a different point of view. Let's say that after Norma's love affair with your father ended, Tod latched onto you. Maybe you two went from being pals to lovers. To disguise that relationship, Norma became your public love-interest. But she won't marry you until you get your inheritance. For that to happen Tod had to get rid of your father. And that would have worked if you hadn't gotten so scared about the lion and then had to go on a canned hunt and involve all kinds of people and bring your own eligibility to inherit into question.

"Tod had to adjust his plans. When you got back from Africa you inherited a million in bonds from your mother. Isn't that when your drug and gambling problems increased exponentially? Tod used your money to buy drugs. Almost a million bucks is gone. Where? You didn't use a million in drugs. You financed his drug business. He's not a user, and you've become an addict. He says he was only trying to help you curtail your habit... that he was rationing the drugs to you. Everybody thinks he's some kind of hero for that. But why did he need all those disposable phones for your personal use? He thinks that nobody can accuse him of being a dealer because his listed phone records are clean and it's Norma who acts as his mule. Have you asked yourself why he needed all those phones?"

"He was being careful, that's all."

"Careful of whom? Jackson. Think! Stop being so damned gullible. When Norma's marriage to your father failed, and when killing your dad also failed, he had to invent another plan. He had to get power over you one way or the other. He made you dependent on him for drugs. But then you became so erratic that he needed something more... something that he could really hold over your head. I'm betting that he got it, and now he's got to kill your uncle before your uncle or the courts can act to disinherit you."

"Kill my father and then my uncle? That's insane."

"Tod is being questioned by the police right now. He got your uncle to hire him... yes, he told him and his attorney that all he was guilty of was trying to wean you off drugs. Your uncle believed him and paid his bail and his attorney's fee. You were jailed. Tod was treated like a hero. Your uncle hired him to help move your stuff out of the house, but Douglass intervened and prevented that. So this morning Tod shows up at your house with his arm in a sling because he says that he hurt himself. He and Charles are going to drive to the Poconos to set up the summer camp. George figured that Tod's plan was to unbuckle his seat belt because it was hurting his injured shoulder and then, when the mountain road was in a dangerous part, he'd turn the wheel and send the car over the edge and he'd jump out. When we finally got the pieces put together we called your uncle and sure enough, they were heading into the dangerous part of the road and Tod had just claimed that his shoulder was hurting him so much that he had to release his seat-belt. Charles no longer trusts Tod. He's outside conferring with your attorney.

"A police doctor is checking Tod's shoulder and the police are questioning him about his drug operation. Wake up, Jackson! In case the plan to marry Norma fell through, he needed some other kind of insurance that you'd still give him what he wanted. Blackmail? What was he holding over your head?"

"Nothing! Tod loves me!"

It suddenly occurred to Akara that Norma's marriage wasn't the only possible nuptial. "Wait a minute... Did Tod ask you to marry him?"

"I don't have to answer that."

"Yes, you do. Jesus, Jackson. Wake up! You need to tell us what he's been up to."

"He did ask. When we got back from Africa it was all over the news that homosexual marriages were becoming legal, so he did ask me; but I said No. I didn't want to go that route."

"Then what is it? Is he married to someone else? In love with someone else?"

"No! I just don't love Tod that way. Sex is one thing. Love is something else."

"I know," Akara said quietly.

"I just said it was too soon after my father's death and my brother's legal troubles. How would that look?" He began to cry. "I loved my dad. I really did."

"So if you turned Tod down, he had to find another way to get you under his thumb. So what is it? What's he got on you? A sex tape? A cheating scandal? An old embarrassing kind of teenage crime? Until we find out what it is, your problems are not going to be solved. I will keep your confidence, but you've got to tell me."

Jackson looked away. Akara waited. When Jackson turned back he said simply, "Vehicular manslaughter. I was drunk and killed a guy in Trenton. I fled the scene."

"When was this?"

"January 9th, 2013."

Akara got out his iPad. He connected to his computer in the temple and began to access various sites. "There were no hit-and-run fatalities on January 9th, 2013 in Trenton. He checked the 10th, 11th, and 12th. "Do you know the name of the person you hit?"

"Augusto DeMaio. d-e-m-a-i-o. He didn't die right away."

Augusto DeMaio, age 34, was instantly killed in a hit and run accident at the corner of 41st Avenue and Truman Boulevard, Trenton, New Jersey, on January 15, 2013, at 8:05 p.m. He was DOA at Trenton General." He turned the iPad around for Jackson to read it. "January 9th was a Wednesday. January 15th was a Tuesday. Are you sure you hit a guy on a Wednesday?"

"Yes, I'm sure. We scored some coke that day. It was the first time we had used that dealer. It was the 9th... around 11 p.m. Wednesday night. I hit the guy!"

Akara typed in a few more commands. "Maybe he was drunk too, and he just got up and walked away. He obviously wasn't hurt that badly since he was walking home intoxicated on the 15th. You didn't kill anybody."

"Yeah. I read his obituary too in the Trenton papers. He died nearly a week after I hit him."

"I'm not accessing the stupid obituaries now. I'm looking at the medical examiner's records and a police accident report. He was hit by a stolen pickup truck that was later abandoned three blocks away." He turned the iPad around again to show Jackson. "Here's the report. Read it for yourself."

Jackson wiped his eyes and read the report on the screen. Then he lay back on his bed and shuddered. "I don't believe it. This is a trick!"

"Believe it! What happened on the 9th?"

"After I hit the guy, Tod made me stop, and then he went back and looked at the body. He said he was 'as good as dead... his head's bashed in.' I hit the man as he was trying to unlock his car door. While Tod was looking at him, I wrote down his license number. I learned his name and told Tod. A couple of days later Tod showed me the obits and then after the funeral he took me in his car to the cemetery and showed me his grave. I saw that there was a six day difference between when I hit him and when he died. Tod said, 'He must have been in good physical shape to hang on for six days in that condition.' I can't believe this! He was my best friend! He loved me. He killed my dad to protect me."

"What? Protect you from what?"

"He said my dad met with a guy who told him about the scene I made at the breakfast table and that I had killed the lion in a canned hunt. My dad was so embarrassed that he was going to set sail immediately and leave me in Mozambique. Tod said he couldn't let him do that. He loved me too much. That's why he lied about Gordon's argument."

"How did he kill your father?"

"He said he made it as painless as possible. He drugged his coffee with chloral hydrate and while it was taking effect, he hooked up the dinghy's motor. There's a railing all the way around the schooner, but it's got gates in it that open. My dad was unconscious, sitting in a chair near one of the gates. Tod opened the gate and pushed him over the side. Then he lowered a rope ladder and climbed down into the dinghy and tied my dad's body to the side. He took Gordon's Browning, and when he got far enough out to sea, he untied my dad and shot him because he didn't want to risk having him wake up and be attacked by sharks. Then he came back to the ship, tied up the dinghy, climbed back up the rope ladder and closed the gate." He bit his lip. "Tod killed my dad to protect me! How do you think that makes me feel?" He began to sob so violently that the infirmary nurse came to the bedside. Akara assured her he'd be fine as he gave Jackson a handful of tissues.

As soon as the sobbing subsided, Akara said, "Jackson... listen to me. Your father was killed on the day you went to Chimoio. Gordon was in his cabin all day after they got back from the aborted fishing trip. The Browning .375 that belonged to your father was kept in Gordon's cabin. Tod had to get the rifle out of his cabin while they were fishing... *which was long before you even killed the lion*. He had already planned to kill your father just to expedite your inheritance. And for all you know Tod also went back and killed the guy you thought you hit in Trenton."

"He told me that if we were married he wouldn't have to testify against me."

"And you still refused? Good for you. He is one evil dude. Maybe he was hoping you wouldn't have to testify against him!"

"What am I going to do?"

"Tell your lawyer the entire truth. He'll know how you should maneuver Tod into talking about your father's death and also the death of the guy in Trenton. Douglass will tell you to do whatever he thinks it's in your best interest to do. I won't say a word. Just tell the truth to Douglass."

"Will I have to go back to Mozambique?"

"They probably want you to pay a fine for your illegal lion hunt. And maybe for pubic intoxication. You can probably pay it by check. Douglass can handle it."

"All right. Tell Mr. Douglass to come back here to tell me what I need to do."

"Gotcha'." Akara got up to leave. Then he turned and made a blessing sign. "Go in peace, my son."

WEDNESDAY, JUNE 26, 2013

Cecelia Smith regarded it as a challenge worthy of her talent and skill to yield to Sonya's plea that the wedding be held in the evening. The portico was ablaze with candles in hurricane lamps, white satin bows, and cattleya orchids.

Tarleton's foyer was decorated to look like a chapel. At the far end of the hall, where several of Cecelia's ancestral portraits hung, a stained glass panel, illuminated from behind, had been installed. In front of it she placed an altar filled with candles and orchids, and a wide *prie dieu* for the bride and groom. Chairs were set in place on either side of the central aisle. Satin bows from which boughs of orchids cascaded were fixed to the aisle-chairs. Society photographers who knew better than to violate Cecelia's rule to photograph only the bride's good side came prepared to see the extravaganza. A sextet of musicians was hired to play Bach and Vivaldi.

The caterers were ordered to maintain absolute silence during the ceremony. The bride, too embarrassed to go searching for a wedding gown where there would be other brides "ready to gape" at her, accepted Lilyanne's suggestion that she try on the new Irish lace gown with the high neckline that Lily had gotten for her own wedding three years before - and had never worn. Lily had had the dress hemmed; but since Sonya was taller than Lily, the hem merely had to be let down to its original length. The sleeves were long and Lily was secretly able to secure the bridal bouquet, hundreds of tiny cascading orchids, to her prosthetic hand. Sonya's face was surrounded by the same tiny orchids that marked the securing edge of the lace veil.

Martin Mazzavini and his grandfather flew in for the ceremony, as did Adam Chang and Jake Renquist who, unaware of each other's purpose, flew in from Honolulu on the same plane. Chang's parents, who lived only a few miles away, also attended. Beryl's son Jack was home from school. He attended with Groff Eckersley and Lionel and Alicia Eckersley. Akara came with a member of the sangha who once had brought him baklava every day. Willem deVries came as Beryl's date. The Chinese consul came from Seattle with the Maitlins and Margaret Cioran. Cecelia calculated that at most they would have thirty guests. They had twenty-eight.

Beryl wore a conservative gown and Jack and Groff wore evening clothes - the first that Jack had ever owned. It was an intimate but glittering affair. All of the women present, except the bride and Beryl, wore an excessive amount of diamonds. Lilyanne wore a green silk satin sheath and the diamond and emerald jewelry for which her family had become famous. George, peeking into the preparation room and seeing her look so beautiful and so much more mature, realized for the first time that he was not merely infatuated with a girl, but was impossibly in love with a woman... someone else's woman.

The music began, and the maid of honor, looking indomitable as only Sylvia Maitlin could look, walked serenely at the head of the procession. The Chinese consular official escorted the bride down the aisle.

George remembered the first time he had seen Sonya Lee... resplendent in a wide black brimmed hat that let red poppies insouciantly tease her ear lobe. She was stunning then... and she was still stunning. "She's still got it," he whispered to Sensei as Sylvia lifted Sonya's veil. "Yes," Sensei answered, "'it' and also my soul."

George had told Sensei that as a wedding present he and Akara were going to buy a row house that was between the temple and the office so that Akara could move into it with his "computer stuff." The honeymooners were going to spend several weeks at the Smith's Cape May, New Jersey residence. When they returned, the entire upstairs temple residence would be ready for them. Then, after the new house was remodeled to the bride's specifications, they would switch places and Akara would be the temple's resident priest.

The ceremony, performed jointly by a retired judge with whom Everett played golf and by one of Sensei's old Buddhist teachers, was over in thirty minutes. The music played triumphantly and Sanford announced that dinner in the dining hall would be served. Place cards with the names inscribed by a calligrapher marked the places at the table where everyone except George began to sit.

Lilyanne approached Beryl. "Where's George?"

"I don't think he intended to stay for dinner. He's really trying to keep to his diet."

"Baloney." She grabbed her car keys and hurried out the back door to the area in which he had parked his pickup truck.

George, having arrived early, had been partially blocked by cars that arrived later. He was moving back and forth, gently turning his truck to ease it out of the narrow space left to him. He was nearly free of it when Lilyanne drove her Jaguar behind his truck and parked, completely blocking his escape.

He opened the truck door and stepped down onto the ground. Had she been a stranger, he would have been annoyed but his tone and his question would have been civil. He'd have asked if perhaps she had not noticed that he was trying to back out of the space. But she was no stranger and so he furiously asked, "What the hell do you think you're doing?"

Lilyanne turned off the ignition and got out of her car. "You're the detective. Try. Really try to figure it out. By your fifth guess you might actually hit the right answer." She tapped her forehead and pretended to imitate him. "Perhaps this lady is trying to prevent me, Former Police Lieutenant Wagner, Homicide, from leaving. Can that be it?"

"Try guessing this: how many RPMs will this truck require to push that little white car out of its way?"

"Are you so childish that you would walk out of your best friend's wedding reception? Oh, yes... that's what Former Police Lieutenant Wagner does when he's scared. He starts running!"

"Running? Isn't that what you're supposed to be doing right now? Running to your husband? Move the car!"

"I don't have a husband! And don't tell me what to do!"

"I won't tell you to move your car, but if you don't move it I'm gonna push it out of the way with my 8 cylinder 4-wheel drive truck. I finished playing games with you a long time ago, Lady! *Move the car!*"

Beryl, Akara, and Everett Smith, alerted to the possible problem, exited the back door and stood at the side of the parking area, watching.

Lilyanne got in her car and backed it up far enough for George to continue backing out of the space. She waited until he swung the pickup in an arc to point it towards the driveway. Then she floored the jaguar and hit it 'T-bone' in the passenger's side. Instantly, both airbags deployed. "*Not the Jag!*" Akara shouted.

George, momentarily stunned, got out of the pick up and, seeing smoke coming from the Jag, stumbled to it and opened the driver's side door. Lilyanne, her nose bleeding, fell out, seemingly unconscious. "Get her out before the car explodes!" Everett shouted, running towards them.

George picked her up. "Look what she's done to my truck! Your daughter is insane."

"I'll take care of your truck! But please get her into the house! Go up the kitchen stairs," Everett ordered. "Let's not upset the other guests." George carried her into the kitchen and up the servants' stairs to the upstairs parlor. "Take her back to her room," Everett said, turning to Beryl. "Should we let Cecelia know?"

"I think she's busy enough. Let's see if Lily is seriously hurt."

George had never been inside her bedroom. "Which door is it?" he growled.

"The next one with the potted palm outside." Akara moved ahead and opened the door so that George could carry her into the room. Lily's face was on top of George's shoulder. She looked at her father, squinted her eyes, and with a flick of her wrist indicated that he should leave them alone. Then she resumed being unconscious.

Beryl had not seen the gesture. She had gone into the bathroom to get a wet washcloth to wipe the blood from Lily's nose. As soon as she handed it to George, Everett pulled her away and with a quick nod of his head, indicated that they should leave. "We'll be out here if you need us," Beryl said. Everyone went into the hallway. Sanford, the majordomo, joined them. Beryl shut the door and then stooped to peek through the keyhole. Everyone stopped to listen.

George knelt beside the bed and wiped the blood from her face. "Is my nose broken?" she whispered.

He put her nose between his thumb and index finger and wiggled it. "No."

"You love your minx. I can tell."

"I was afraid that you had gotten hurt in the collision. Do you know how much paperwork that would have been for me?"

"When are we getting married? Could it please be before my parents die of old age?"

"I don't care when or if they die. You are no concern of mine."

"You promised to marry me!"

"I promised you shit!"

"That's right," she whimpered, "be vulgar. A sacred moment in time... a proposal of marriage... and you have to spoil all my memories of it with your vulgarity."

"Well, excuuuuse me! I most assuredly do not want to taint your sacred memories with my vulgarity!"

"Then take it back."

"Take what back?"

"That you promised me... you know what!"

"That I promised you shit?"

Beryl, her eye to the keyhole, Akara, Everett, and Sanford all listened and looked at each other quizzically.

"Yes. Take it back!"

"All right. I didn't promise you shit."

"Aaahhh," Lilyanne wailed, "you did it again!" She began to whimper as tears rolled down her cheeks. "*You spoiled a precious moment... with fecal material.*"

George put his hands over his face and bent forward until his knuckles touched the carpet. "Fecal material?" he whispered. His shoulders were shaking. Beryl could not tell if he was laughing, crying, or praying.

He was, in fact, doing all three. "My God. My God," he pleaded. "What terrible sin did I commit that I should deserve this?"

Lilyanne slipped out of bed and ran her fingers through his hair as she cradled his head. "Don't ask God. He's the One who gave you to me, and you're non-returnable." She rubbed her cheek against his face. "Pick a date," she whispered in his ear as she began to give him little kisses.

He groaned. "Is there no escape?" He groaned again.

"None. None whatsoever. You are in eternal bondage. Now, what should I tell everyone about our plans?"

"I don't care. Tell them whatever you want."

"Good. I'm glad you've decided to be reasonable." She turned and looked at the door. "Daddy!" she called. "George proposed and I said, 'Yes.'"

-30-